With his ha   "I feel your desire, Kathleen

A small gas   She felt as though he was reaching into her mind and becoming part of her. That insight stunned her, frightened her, because she let no one get close to her. And she couldn't control this uniting of emotions, of souls, that went beyond anything she had ever experienced.

Kathleen's hold on him tightened, her fingertips turning white. One of his hands slipped lower and came to rest over her heart. With his other hand he placed her splayed fingers over his heart. Its rapid, rhythmic beat matched hers, rushing into her, filling her with his desire.

"They beat as if one," he whispered, the declaration binding her to him as if their hearts were truly united.

"I don't understand what is happening to me. Why do I feel what you feel?"

He grinned, a lopsided lifting of one corner of his mouth. "Neither do I. For all sane purposes I should never have brought you here that first night."

"Then why did you?" The inquiry came out breathless, barely audible.

But he heard and smiled. "That's a good question."

"But one you aren't going to answer?"

He buried his hands in the long strands of her hair and looked into her eyes. "No."

"What do you want from me? And don't tell me it's that you want me to leave the jungle. That's not why you brought me here that first night."

Before Kathleen could react, he crushed his mouth into hers, holding her head still while the grinding pressure of his lips demanded her response. She wanted to push him away, to scrub away his touch because she felt her very nature slipping from her with each second his kiss claimed her. And yet, she wanted to dissolve into his toughened ardent brand with one of her own.

HOLD ONTO THE NIGHT

Shauna Michaels

HOLD ONTO THE NIGHT
Published by ImaJinn Books, a division of ImaJinn

First Printing July, 2000

ISBN: 1-893896-11-0

PUBLISHER'S NOTE:
This book is a work of fiction. Names, characters, places and incidents are products of the author's imagination or are used fictitiously. Any resemblance to actual events or locales or persons, living or dead, is entirely coincidental.

Books are available at quantity discounts when used to promote products or services. For information please write to: Marketing Division, ImaJinn Books, P.O. Box 162, Hickory Corners, MI 49060-0162, or call toll free 1-877-625-3592.

Cover design by Patricia Lazarus

ImaJinn Books, a division of ImaJinn
P.O. Box 162, Hickory Corners, MI 49060-0162
Toll Free: 1-877-625-3592
http://www.imajinnbooks.com

DEDICATION

To the best critique group
(Ada, Judy, Mary Jane, Cathy and Laura)
This book is for you.

Note from ImaJinn Books

Dear Readers,

Thank you for buying this book. The author has worked hard to bring you a captivating tale of love and adventure.

In the months ahead, watch for our fast-paced, action-packed stories involving ghosts, psychics and psychic phenomena, witches, vampires, werewolves, angels, reincarnation, futuristic in space or on other planets, futuristic on earth, time travel to the past, time travel to the present, and any other story line that will fall into the "New-Age" category.

The best way for us to give you the types of books you want to read is to hear from you. Let us know your favorite types of "New-Age" romance. You may write to us or any of our authors at: ImaJinn Books, P.O. Box 162, Hickory Corners, MI 49060-0162, or e-mail us at imajinnbooks@worldnet.att.net.

And visit our web site at: http://www.imajinnbooks.com

Chapter One

Something wasn't right about the night.

Dr. Kathleen Dawson could feel it deep in the marrow of her bones. The jungle was too quiet, the Indian helpers too agitated. She settled back on the log by the fire, her thoughts troubled. A nagging ache stiffened the muscles of her shoulders and neck.

Scanning the area, she shivered. The darkness beyond the camp reminded her of a black curtain, hiding menacing possibilities on the other side. Finally her gaze settled on Santo, sitting across from her, his bronzed face cast in the reddish glow from the fire. His features suddenly seemed sinister, fueling her vivid imagination.

"I love the rain forest during the day, but it certainly is a different story at night," Kathleen said in Spanish, talking to still disquieting thoughts that were conjuring up all kinds of evil images out of the black of night.

"Stay close to the fire." Santo shifted uneasily from one side to the other, his hands extended toward the flames, his gaze darting about as though trying to see through the dark.

"A tribe of headhunters could be lurking out there." Indicating the jungle beyond the fire with a wave of her hand,

Kathleen forced a lightness into her voice, but her childhood fear of the night pushed to the foreground.

"Or the Jaguar Man. He likes the night."

"Jaguar Man?" She lifted her hand to rub across her knitted brow, feeling the wet sheen of the moisture-laden air on her skin. "Wasn't that who your helpers were whispering about earlier?"

"Yes. They aren't happy. This place is too close to *his* territory. And it has begun to rain a lot earlier than it should. Not a good sign."

Kathleen straightened, alert at her Dalco guide's tone that held a warning and a touch of fear. "This Jaguar Man myth won't interfere with why we are here, will it?"

"Myth?"

"Of course. There's no such thing as a man who is a jaguar by day."

Standing, Santo glanced at his helpers. "They think so."

"Do you?"

He frowned. "I may now live in the capital and work for a big company like Dalco, but I was born in the jungle. It's hard to forget where you came from."

"Then you don't think it's a myth?"

Santo stared down at her, then looked toward his helpers. "They think he comes in the night to protect the jungle. It's his, and he tolerates no trespassers touching his home."

Santo's whispered words flowed like the wind through the forest, bringing a chill to Kathleen while ripples of fear vibrated through her.

The Indian smiled, his gaze sliding away. "Do not worry. You are safe with us."

"Yeah," Kathleen mumbled as Santo walked away, apprehensive because his smile hadn't reached his eyes. "Then why do I feel like I'm being watched? That everything is out of my control?"

Hugging her arms to her, Kathleen tried to shake off the dread forging a strong hold on her. But her conversation with Santo only strengthened the ominous feeling that something wasn't right about the night. The rain had finally stopped an hour before, and she heard the dripping water rolling off the leaves above and splashing onto the forest floor below. She breathed in the clean, fresh smell after a downpour. Santo had assured her the canoes used to get her here were secured on the river. Everything should be all right, but deep inside she knew that wasn't true.

As she stared at the flames devouring the pieces of wood, she thought of her home in Texas and how very different Costa Sierra was from Dallas. She had once referred to her hometown as a jungle, but it wasn't anything like this. She glanced at the wall of darkness and wished she were back in Dallas, where everything was predictable and orderly. In her world of science, logic and rationality ruled, not superstitious stories of a Jaguar Man who ruled the jungle, protecting it from outsiders at all costs.

"Well, Kathleen, you wanted to come to Costa Sierra. So now, you'd better make the best of it and go to sleep. Tomorrow will be another long day," she said out loud, comforted by the sound of her own voice in the eerie stillness. Standing, she rolled her shoulders to ease the stiffness and headed for her tent, leaving the flap open to let in the firelight—and to feel nearer to the only other humans she had seen in over a day.

Her hammock swayed while she positioned herself in it, the canvas molding itself to her backside. Pulling the mosquito netting over her, she closed her eyes and drew in deep breaths of the dank, damp air. As she listened to the noise of the jungle, it sounded different, not like it had the previous evening down river. Subdued, she thought, as if the animals and insects were waiting, silent in their vigil.

Waiting for what?

She surveyed the campsite through the open tent flap. The Indians were settled in their hammocks, sleeping. The fire blazed and would for a few more hours if it didn't start raining again. She could see nothing beyond the mantle of darkness. The feeling, however, still persisted that her life was about to change.

For a long time Kathleen watched until her eyelids grew heavy, and she yawned. "This is ridiculous." She had to get some sleep because tomorrow, after traveling for days to this remote part of the rain forest, she would begin her search.

With a sigh she settled in the hammock and tried to wipe her mind of all thoughts except counting backward from one thousand. The last number she remembered was nine hundred sixty as sleep descended like the night in the jungle, quickly, silently.

***

He walked soundlessly through the campsite toward the tent that held the woman, his every sense alert for any change in his surroundings. Nothing escaped him, not the slightest movement, not the slightest sound.

Yanking back the mosquito netting, he stared at the woman in the hammock, studying her features, serene in sleep. Her feminine scent blended with the other more powerful aromas of the jungle, pulling him closer. Her long auburn hair framed her delicately molded face. Her skin was creamy with a touch of rose in it.

Drawn to her despite his need not to be, he caressed a strand of hair away from her cheek, a tingling awareness of the woman invading him. Startled, he yanked his hand away. He hadn't touched a woman like this since—A tightness in his gut twisted painfully, prodding memories forward.

He forced his gaze away from the woman and around to inspect the campsite. The equipment she used was in a nearby tent. The Indians lay in their hammocks, oblivious to his coming, as he knew they would be. Returning his regard to her, he clenched his hands, determined to hold onto his control. She represented civilization, a world so far removed from his, a world forbidden to him now.

Shutting down all emotions, he withdrew a dart from his pouch and pierced the flesh of her neck. She jerked, trying to twist away. He clamped his hand over her mouth and held her still in her hammock until the sedative took effect. Then he bent over and scooped her into his arms. With a supreme effort, he blocked out all feelings and headed out of the camp, her petite body nestled in his embrace.

***

A haze clung to Kathleen's thoughts, unwilling to release its grip. She struggled to push the mist back, to reach toward the light. Her eyes flew open as a screeching sound pierced the air. She bolted up, and the world spun. Moaning, she sank onto a soft bed of broad leaves, shutting out the whirling picture threatening to shove her back into unconsciousness.

The sound knifed the air again, sending a chill down her spine. This time she opened her eyes slowly and surveyed her surroundings from a reclining position. A dank, smoky scent embraced the air. A fire lit the rock walls of a cave, strewing spectral shadows onto their facade. Around the large cavern, which Kathleen estimated was a hundred feet across, lit torches cast the limestone formations in an eerie glow that made her shiver in the warm air.

For a few seconds she was transfixed by the beauty of the stalactite and stalagmite structures like stone icicles until she realized that someone lived in the cavern. Several pieces of crude furniture—two stools, a table, the platform she lay on—littered the cave. On the table sat eating utensils, bowls, and plates. A large trunk stood against the wall opposite her, a lone sign of civilization amidst this primitive environment.

Where am I? Who brought me here? Why?

As the questions flittered through her mind, she heard the noise again and turned her head until she found the source of the unearthly sound. A howler monkey stood not five feet away. It stared at her while rocking from side to side, its arms swinging about madly.

Is this how Jane had felt?

Praying she was dreaming and that any second she would awaken, Kathleen looked beyond the monkey. That was when she saw the elongated, ghostly image looming on the wall and spied the man, poised in front of the fire. His sudden, soundless appearance was like a phantom in a horror story.

Her gaze traveled up his tall frame, noting his leather clad feet, his bare legs that revealed muscular thighs, his flat stomach covered partially by a loincloth made of animal skins, and his broad, bronzed chest that spoke of a man who was in superb physical condition. Involuntarily, her pulse tripled in reaction to his magnificent physique. As she fought to remain calm, her gaze continued upward, taking in his long black hair, his wide shoulders, his tight frown, and strong, unyielding jaw. She stopped her perusal when she looked into his eyes. They were the color of burnished gold—intense and penetratingly unnerving. Swallowing her gasp, she moved back until she felt the coolness of the cave's stone wall.

She opened her mouth to say something, but no words would come. Her heart pounded against her rib cage while blood roared in her ears. Frantically, she scanned the cave once more, hoping there was someone else nearby. No one. She was alone with a man who looked like Tarzan and was perfectly at home in this primeval setting.

"Who are you?" she finally managed to ask, her voice quavering. Her hands crushed the soft bedding of leaves, their scent wafting to her as a reminder she had left civilization behind and had stepped into an alien world.

Eyes of gold narrowed on her. The silence of his stone lair was only broken by the chattering monkey. Its sound ate away at her nerves, tautened to their limits.

She would not allow him to intimidate her with his silence. "Why am I here?" Her voice grew stronger as her anger took over and thrust her fear to the background.

The monkey stopped howling at the force of her words and scurried away. The man, however, stood with his feet braced apart, his arms rigid at his sides. His look impaled her. She felt as though she had intruded on him—that her being in the cave was her fault. No! She wasn't to blame.

"I asked you a question. Who are you?" Her anger, mounting at the momentary feeling of guilt, laced her words.

Refusing to lie on the bed another moment, she scrambled to her feet, ignoring the dizzy feeling caused by the quick movement. She was determined to show no fear as she met his unwavering regard with one of her own. Two could play this game, she thought, as she let her gaze journey down the tall length of him, making sure insolence was clear in her expression.

The silence continued to reign. She measured him; he measured her.

"My name is not important," he finally said, his deep voice rough, as if he weren't used to speaking.

"Where am I?"

"In a cave."

Her laugh was bitter. "Tell me something I don't already know."

"You're my guest."

"Am I free to leave?"

"No."

The finality of the whispered word quivered in the humid air, and it took all of her effort not to quake. "Then your definition of 'guest' is quite different from mine."

He said nothing to her retort, but his golden gaze continued to drill into her, accusing in its regard. She shifted uncomfortably, her fear returning as though it were a snake slithering its way up her body to twine about her in a death grip.

Clenching her teeth, Kathleen hugged herself, determined not to look away from the silent battle raging between them. The moisture-rich air cloaked her in a thin layer of dampness at the same time she shook from a cold deep in her bones, chilling her.

"Why am I here?"

Again silence saturated the cavern.

"I have a right to know why you kidnapped me," she said, hating the hint of desperation in her voice. She stared at his immovable body, balanced as if ready to fight, and she gritted her teeth in frustration. "Please."

Nothing in his expression gave any indication that he had even heard her.

She finally looked away from his burning gaze and searched the chamber for a way out. She found a dark passage near her and, without another thought, raced toward it. She expected to hear him behind her, but only silence followed her into the corridor. An ebony shroud fell around her, its mantle concealing all light except the faint flames of his fire. Kathleen stopped, flinging her arms out in front. As she explored with her fingertips what lay ahead, she felt the cool wall of the passageway and slowly inched forward.

She glanced back toward the light, sure she would see him silhouetted in the entrance. Nothing. Strangely, that made her fear mushroom. Turning back, she groped for a way out of her stone prison, each step she took taking her farther and farther away from the light and into a pitch darkness that began to frighten her more than the man in the cavern.

When she came upon yet another twist in the passage, she realized she had two choices of which way to go. Her fear of the dark caused her heart to pound. She was sure the man could hear its sound all the way back to the high ceilinged chamber. Her hammering heartbeat seemed to fill the cave with its warning to go no further, to turn back and take her chances with the stranger.

She sank down onto the dirt floor and leaned back against the cavern wall. Curling her legs against her chest, she clasped her arms about them and laid her head on her knees. Why hadn't he come after her?

Because he knew there wasn't a way out. She was trapped in a dark pit of hell.

She looked about her, trying to see something —anything. But not even the firelight reached her surroundings. Suddenly she was confused. Which way was back to him?

Tears stung her eyes, but she refused to let them fall. She would wait until morning. Maybe then she would find her way out. But even as she thought that, she knew her chances were slim that she'd even know when dawn came. In fact, it could be morning now. She didn't know how long she had lain on the bed of leaves. Hours? Days?

Closing her eyes, she acknowledged the exhaustion weaving its way through her. The past few days of traveling to Costa Sierra and then setting up camp were taking their toll. She would just rest her eyes for a few minutes, then try again to escape.

***

He followed her scent through the labyrinth and found her slumped against the wall, hugging her legs, her eyes closed in sleep. Her long hair, like flames of a fire, flowed over her limbs, brushing the tops of her ankles. After placing the torch he carried into a crevice, he knelt beside her. Hesitantly he reached out, touching her hair. Taking the fiery strands within his grasp, he let them fall away, the feel of her hair soft against his skin. For a few minutes he allowed his fascination with her to envelope him in needs he thought were buried. They sliced into him, invoking the pain of remembering what he could no longer have.

Why had he brought her to the cave? He had never brought anyone here before. He didn't have an answer; he only knew he felt compelled to try to talk her into leaving Costa Sierra rather than using his usual tactics. Unexpectedly he had been touched by her fear, and he'd wanted to protect her.

His jaw hardened. That part of his life was over, gone forever. He refused to allow this woman to sway him from his course, to permit her fear to change his mind about what he must do. He wouldn't let her feelings touch him, to remind him of what he had been forced to leave behind. He could not go back.

As he bent toward her, his hair fell forward to mingle with hers, black on red. Lifting her, he smelled the womanly aroma that had drawn him to her. Her fresh scent reminded him of the jungle after a cleansing rainstorm. Settling her against his chest, he tried to ignore the tightening of his groin, the flow of emotions from her, but he couldn't. Her fear and sadness were so strong and overwhelming. She snuggled into his embrace, sharpening his constriction to a throbbing ache.

Sucking in deep breaths, he closed his eyes for a few seconds and fought for control. He strived to push her warmth from his heart. Slowly a calmness descended, and he detached himself emotionally from the situation—from the woman—as he had learned so successfully to do.

When he was in control again, he acknowledged it had been a mistake to bring her to his home.

He headed back to the cavern where he lived. He laid the woman on his bed, then stepped away, toward the fire's warmth. He felt cold, as though the ice about his heart had spread to encompass his whole body.

He stared into the blaze and instantly thought of the woman. Why did the outside world have to intrude now? He wanted no reminders of a past best forgotten. He balled his hands into tight fists. It was becoming harder and harder for him to shut himself off from those memories. He had managed in the past by keeping a tight rein on his emotions. With her he was afraid he had lost the ability to control his feelings.

***

When Kathleen opened her eyes, she felt the softness of leaves beneath her. She smelled the aroma of burning wood, heard the crackling of the fire, the quiet movement of *him*. He had permitted her to flee, knowing she wouldn't go far. Again her anger swelled.

Carefully she sat up, drawing the man's attention to her. The keenness in his gaze as it raked over her body robbed her of breath. For a brief moment she thought she glimpsed regret and pain in his eyes, but he quickly concealed his thoughts behind a blank expression and turned back to the fire, its smoke curling up to the ceiling and disappearing through a crack.

Kathleen brought her fingers up to her temples to massage them. The pounding behind her eyes increased its tempo. She had to be dreaming this. Tomorrow she would awaken in her tent with sunshine streaming in through its flap, and this would all be a figment of her imagination. This didn't happen in the real world.

She watched him put some wood on the fire. The ripple of his muscles as he executed each movement was mesmerizing. No doubt about it. She had thought up a perfect man. What in the world was her subconscious telling her? That her life was too devoid of male companionship? Her one serious relationship, her disastrous marriage, had ended in an ugly divorce. Since then, she had pledged all her energies toward her career, something she could govern with cool logic and a no-nonsense approach to life. Emotions had a way of spinning out of control, leaving you grasping for stability.

"These caves are a maze. You can't freely roam around in them. People have died in them," he said, prodding a burning log with a stick.

"You've made your point. But don't expect my thanks for saving me."

He threw her a glance that froze her with his scorn, but said not a word.

"Will you tell me why I'm here as your—*guest*?"

He dropped the stick into the fire and swivelled toward her to spear her with his sharp gaze, the coldness in his eyes still there. "To warn you to leave."

She shot to her feet. "Leave? I just arrived."

He slowly stood and approached her. "Why are you here?"

She didn't owe him any explanation. She gave him a frosty look as her gaze traversed his tall frame. His power and anger were conveyed in his stance, his expression, the very essence of him. Lifting her chin, she stared into his burnished gold eyes, fighting the feeling of being pulled into their depths, of becoming lost in their rich intensity.

"What are you looking for?"

His question cut into the thick air. She swallowed to ease the tight ache in her throat, trying to keep her surprise from showing. This man was more than he seemed and certainly no Tarzan, raised in the jungle by apes. He was educated. It was evident in his speech and his bearing.

"Whatever I'm looking for is none of your business."

"Everything that happens here is my business."

"Why? Who are you?"

"I'm just a man protecting his home."

Just a man? Protecting his home? His declaration produced a quickening in her pulse. "People will come looking for me," she said with a bravado she wished she truly felt because, in her excitement to explore the jungle, she had come ahead of the rest of the team. They wouldn't arrive for several weeks.

"I've become quite good at discouraging people who are looking."

Kathleen swallowed hard, but her throat constricted with fear, and her head throbbed with tension. "How?"

For the first time he smiled, but it left his eyes as cold as before. The short distance between them pulsed with his virility, conveyed in his stance, in the hard, chiseled features of his face. "Rest assured you're safe from harm so long as you stay in this cave. We're deep inside a mountain, and it's a long way out. I wouldn't try to escape again."

"How do you discourage people? By kidnaping them?" she asked, trying to ignore the threat behind his words.

"I don't have to do anything. The rain has started earlier than usual. You need to leave before you can't."

"This is a rain forest. It rains. I have another eleven or twelve weeks before the rainy season. Plenty of time to do what I need to do."

"Nature doesn't always operate on people's convenient timetables. The river will be impassable soon."

"You're just saying that to get me to leave. Santo hasn't said a thing about the river flooding."

"He's from the city now. He's been away from the jungle too long. I won't permit you to stay. You must leave tomorrow morning." He turned back to the fire. "Are you hungry?"

"Hungry? Why, yes. I didn't eat much tonight," she said, thrown by the shift in conversation to such a mundane topic.

"Yes, I know."

"How?"

"I've been watching you. I don't like surprises, and I never leave anything to chance."

His answer shocked her for a moment. Watching? Again the feeling of danger associated with this man inundated her until she remembered he would know what she knew, that she had nothing really to fear from a phantom of her mind because this had to be a dream.

His probing gaze locked with hers. "Would you like something to eat?"

For a long moment his look stole her voice. Her throat closed about the words she wanted to say as she stared into his eyes, so enthralling, as though he could hypnotize her with them. "Yes," she finally answered when the tension between them pulsated in the air.

As he prepared the food, she tried to ignore him. But she couldn't. She felt a tautness, an enigmatic aura about the man that again produced that sense of peril and something else—something intangible and emphatic. A silent threat charged the air, forcing her to realize she was alone with a man who could overpower her at any moment.

She eased down onto the bed. *This is just a dream. That's the only explanation that is reasonable*, she reminded herself again and tried to relax her stiff muscles, her tightly coiled stomach. She didn't succeed. Her tension gripped her as securely, overwhelmingly as the vines on the jungle's tree trunks.

"Here," he said and walked to her, holding out a wooden plate.

She reached up, her gaze connecting with his. Her hand stopped halfway between them. The molten gold depths of his eyes scorched her where they touched. She swallowed convulsively, a trembling rushing through her.

He thrust the plate into her hand, a scowl wiping the heated expression from his face. Kathleen felt the wintry caress of his look, and fear nibbled at the edges of her mind.

"Eat, then we will talk some more," he commanded, turning away, giving her some space to breathe and get control of her nerves.

He sat near the fire and began to eat his meal with a relish. Kathleen watched for a few moments, almost envying his disregard for civilization. The sound of him licking his fingers was disarming. The sight of his tongue slowly sliding across his lips shoved any anger into the background while she dealt with other feelings rampaging out of control—desires she couldn't believe she was experiencing.

Blushing, she quickly lowered her gaze and stared at her food. Oh, my Lord, she couldn't remember being this affected by a man, not even during her short-lived marriage to Tom. It had to be the heat of the jungle. She just didn't let her emotions reign. But whether she liked it or not, this man had a strange pull on her. She felt bound to him in a way she had never thought possible and it scared her. That feeling, more than anything, convinced her that she had to be dreaming.

She forced her attention to her food. It consisted of unknown plants and fruits, except for a banana which she chose to eat first. Resolved not to look at him while she ate, she kept her gaze lowered even though she felt his on her. It burrowed into her, sweeping away any hunger she had. The banana settled in her stomach like a rock, and she couldn't eat any more.

"I thought you were hungry."

"I was," she whispered, her voice raw with the warring emotions he provoked. She was intrigued by her mythical man at the same time she was repelled, frightened. "I'm not now."

When he put his plate down, Kathleen tensed. Holding her breath, she waited for him to speak.

"Have you thought about what I said about leaving before you can't?"

"No."

His earlier scowl returned, deeper, more menacing. "Why not?"

"Because you aren't real. I didn't come to Costa Sierra to play games with an imaginary man."

He rose, his movements restrained, as though he was afraid to unleash all his power. In three strides he was in front of her and gripping her arms to haul her to her feet. Startled by the quickness of his actions and the sudden surge of his anger, she didn't resist him until he was a breath away and his scent of jungle and man engulfed her. She struggled to twist away, but his hold only tightened as he pulled her against his rock hard body.

One of his hands came up to tangle in the long strands of her hair while the other cupped her face. His gaze bore into her. She couldn't even swallow, so entrapped was she by his fervor, by the desire and anger pouring from his body. Her shock robbed her of all thoughts except her feeling of connection with this man that went beyond the possible.

While she felt herself slipping further out of control, she watched him rein in his emotions as though he could shut a door on his feelings.

"So, you think I'm an imaginary man."

The softly spoken words—no, *threat*—were ominous. Slowly he brushed his roughened thumb across her lips, over and over, making her forget everything but the feel of his skin against hers. Her heartbeat quickened, leaving her lightheaded and clasping him for support. With their gazes still bound, he continued his tactile exploration with a soft caress across her cheek and down her neck. He found the pulse-beat at the base of her throat and laid his thumb over it.

She knew he felt the rapid throb of her blood pounding through her veins asserting her bodily response to him. She was attracted to this stranger, imagined or not, on a primitive level that ridiculed all the control she had mastered over the years. Awash in feelings of passion that she had never experienced, everything familiar to her slid away to be replaced with the unknown.

While his hand clasped the nape of her neck, his thumb drew slow, captivating circles over the place where her pulse vibrated, pulling her closer and closer to him with his magic touch. Her grip on him increased, her fingernails digging into the hard muscles of his shoulders. Suddenly, the emotions he'd held in check while touching her face stroked her, weaving their potency within her, entwining about hers like a lover, until she wasn't certain which were his feelings and which were hers.

Her eyes widened at the emotions—hers and his—that she was experiencing. She tore away from him and distanced herself, unable to believe the intimate connection his touch had produced. It wasn't possible, she silently screamed.

"Do I feel like an imaginary man?"

Oh, my God, this can't be real!

"I want you to know that I am very real."

For a long moment she said nothing as she struggled to piece together each fragment of her composure.

"Have I proved my point?"

"You have a most persuasive way about you. First you kidnap me, and now you manhandle me. What's next?"

He ignored her sarcastic question and waved his hand toward the bed of leaves. "Have a seat."

She looked down at his stone platform bed and shook her head. "I think I'll remain standing. Safer, I believe."

His harsh laugh echoed off the stone walls. "If I had wanted more from you, I wouldn't have had to force myself. I felt your attraction beneath my hand."

A swell of anger flashed through her. She didn't understand any of what was happening to her, least of all the strong impression that they had just bonded on a more intimate level than making love. "Please, just tell me what you have to say that was so important that you took me from my camp."

"The area of the rain forest you want to explore is off limits to you. The Indians who live there are fighting for their lives. White men's diseases have nearly wiped them out. There is only one village of the Xango Indians left. They can't survive another invasion."

"I'm only one person, not an army. I'm just looking for oil."

"And what if you find it? More people will come, an *army* of people. I've seen it before. No matter how hard the Indians try not to have contact with these people, they will be contacted, then the trouble will begin. I won't allow it. And now, with this rain starting, if you don't leave immediately, you will be forced to remain indefinitely."

The prospects of having to stay indefinitely heightened her tension. She couldn't imagine being forced to be with this man for any length of time. "I only have your word for all this. You expect me to trust someone who flaunts the rules of society and takes what he wants?"

"I have warned you. If you ignore me, then I'm not responsible for what happens to you." He turned away and knelt by the fire. Taking a pot from the blaze, he held it up. "Would you like something to drink?"

She blinked, nonplused at the almost civilized question after such a dire threat. "Coffee?"

"No, a special brew I discovered."

She started to refuse, but the icy tentacles of fear still gripped her. With her throat parched, she nodded, as though some unknown force prompted her to accept the drink when she knew she probably shouldn't.

While he poured her some of his brew, she glanced about the high-ceilinged cavern. Even though she had to acknowledge the raw beauty of the two story chamber, she couldn't imagine anyone choosing to live in a cave like an animal, denying the comforts civilization offered.

As Kathleen swung around to face him, she drew in a deep, startled breath. The man was only a foot from her, holding out a wooden cup. His masculine potency electrified the humid air about her, reminding her of the atmosphere right before a thunderstorm. Releasing the captured breath, she hesitantly took the cup from him, and thankfully he moved away as silently as he had approached her. When he returned to the fire, she began to breathe normally again.

Bringing the cup to her lips, she sipped the sweetly flavored liquid and surveyed the room. It was as far removed from her home in Dallas as possible. A few cooking utensils, a couple of stools made out of a tree, a large trunk and a bed of leaves that covered a platform were all that indicated the cavern was occupied.

"Who are you? Why are you here? You're obviously an American." Kathleen cradled the cup between her hands.

"As I said earlier, my name is of no importance."

"Why do you live in a cave?"

"This cavern is quite comfortable. I have everything I want."

Kathleen glanced about, trying to see what was comfortable about stone. "Are you hiding? Are you a criminal?" She yawned. Sitting on the bed, she took another drink of his delicious concoction. She felt light as the wind blowing through the trees. Suddenly, all her fears were gone.

He laughed, a chilling sound. "I wish it were that simple, Kathleen."

Her eyes widened with shock. "You know who I am?" She fought a yawn but couldn't stop it.

"Dr. Kathleen Dawson, geologist for the Dalco Oil Company."

"You went through my papers!" Indignation shoved all other emotions out of the way. He had invaded her privacy like a thief in the night. She grasped onto her anger, trying to use it to clear the haze seeping into her thoughts, but it was becoming so difficult.

He said nothing as he moved nearer. With another yawn she placed the cup on the floor, squinting to try to focus on his large body, to see into those strangely compelling eyes of burnished gold. Everything blurred. Blinking, she rubbed her hands down her face and looked again at him. It appeared as though a dark mist were swallowing him up. As she started to reach out toward him, darkness enveloped her.

Chapter Two

The first sensation Kathleen felt as she came out of a deep sleep was the swaying of the hammock beneath her. The second was the sounds of the jungle, quieted by the fall of rain on her tent's roof.

This isn't a cave. That thought infiltrated into her confused mind as her eyes snapped open and she saw through the mosquito netting to the canvas ceiling above her. *Not rocks.* Dull daylight slanted through the tent flap, casting a dimness on the tarp-covered floor. *Not firelight.*

Clouds of turmoil still clung to the edges of her mind as she swung her legs over the side of the hammock and sat up slowly. She surveyed her surroundings and realized she was where she was supposed to be. But how?

Did I really dream the man? Did I dream being taken? The cave?

With a violent shake of her head, she tried to rid herself of the cobwebs of sleep. Surely then she could make sense out of what was happening.

What kind of game is he playing? Did I dream the man?

A dull ache began to hammer against her temples the more she tried to think about the night before. The man had seemed so real. She could still feel the coldness of his eyes on her, the heated feel of his hands as they had touched her, the power that emanated from him as he had stood a foot from her and had given her the cup. But mostly she could still feel his emotions tangling with hers, becoming one with hers. *Impossible!*

She glanced down at her shaking hands and struggled to reconstruct all the events of the evening past. Bits and pieces filtered through her thoughts. A monkey. A bed of leaves. A maze. A man who had taken her from the campsite. Then why was she here now?

She massaged her temples to ease the intensifying pounding behind her eyes. "It has to be a dream. That makes the most sense."

Always logical, she pushed the bizarre nightmare to the back of her mind, determined to get on with her search. She had an overactive imagination. It had really played a trick on her because of how tired she had been from traveling and hearing the stories about the Jaguar Man.

Standing, she stretched her cramped muscles until she felt limber. That little bit of exertion, however, left exhaustion cleaving to her body like an insect caught in a spider's web. With a glance at her watch she realized she had slept over eight hours. Then why was she so tired? She remembered the frantic attempt to escape the man in her dreams, the draining emotions that had reduced her to exhaustion. But that was only a dream, wasn't it?

"It's the humidity," she muttered, again shaking off the sensation that she had been in a cave the night before. If that had been true, she would still be there. Final. "No more debate," she told herself and wet a washcloth.

After freshening up, she felt better, more prepared to face the long day ahead. Donning a slicker, she left her tent to find Santo. She walked across the camp and shouldered her way past him into the tent where he and his two helpers were waiting out the rain, frowns marring their faces.

"Santo," Kathleen said, holding out the folded map of the area for him to see. "I think we should start looking here and fan outward."

With a scowl he signaled for his two helpers to leave. They hurried out of the tent into the downpour. Seconds later Kathleen lost sight of them behind the gray sheets of rain.

"Is something wrong?"

He shook his head, but his scowl remained as he stared out into the water-drenched jungle.

"Santo, I have to go to that area," she said, pointing to the map again.

"They won't go. They don't like the sign today. You aren't wanted here."

Exasperated, she tunneled her fingers through her long, loose hair. "What sign?"

Santo tossed his head toward the back of the tent. Kathleen followed the direction he indicated and gasped when she saw a skull mounted on a pole sticking up between two hammocks. "Is it—is it?" She swallowed. "What is it?" Her mouth felt bone dry as she stared at the hollowed out eyes, knowing from its shape and size that it wasn't human.

"A jaguar."

"So this was what he meant," she whispered.

Santo became alert. "Who?"

"The man in the cave," she answered without really thinking.

"What man? What cave?"

She focused on Santo's worried face and realized she had said the wrong thing. "It's nothing. Just a dream I had about a man who lived in a cave." She waited a few seconds before adding, "There is no Jaguar Man. It's only a myth."

"Then how do you explain this?" He waved his hand wildly at the skull.

"I—" She tried to come up with a logical explanation and didn't have one, except that her mythical man was real. "I can't." If he was real, she wasn't going to tell Santo. If he was real, then that meant the mingling of their emotions had been real, and she couldn't accept that. That wasn't possible. She was a scientist who believed in logic. But as she thought that, fear gripped her at the implication someone wanted to stop her, someone who could delve deep inside her to her core.

His brown eyes grew round. "You've met the Jaguar Man." Santo took several steps away from her, as though she were contagious and he were afraid to come too close. "He's watching us. That's why the jaguar was spotted near here this morning."

"No, you have it all wrong. I fell asleep and had a dream. That is all. Jaguars are a part of this jungle. That's why you saw one this morning."

"I had heard stories before, but I never really thought—" Santo crossed himself, his eyes huge, his hand over his heart. "Senorita Dawson, you have angered the Jaguar Man. It's rare to see a jaguar unless he wants to be seen."

A heavy mantle of frustration pressed down on her. The hammering inside her skull doubled its time. "That's not possible," she murmured, her shoulders sagging with the imaginary weight of the mantle. She couldn't have the men think there really was a Jaguar Man. "I'm sure I dreamed the man in the cave. That's the only explanation of why I woke up in the camp this morning. Why would he return me to camp if he was really the Jaguar Man and was angry at me being here?" As she spoke to Santo, she began to believe it all had to be a dream or she was going crazy, the humid heat frying her brain.

"But you said—"

Kathleen cut off his words, realizing she had admitted more than she wanted. "Look, all this rain is getting to me. We can wait until it stops, but I want to begin my search as soon as possible," she said with all the authority of the person who was paying these men's wages.

Santo nodded once, his eyes filled with fear.

Kathleen left, racing across the clearing to her tent. Inside she shut out the camp and the men, lighting a lantern to chase away the dim fringe of gloom. Pacing from one end of her tent to the other, she covered the distance in four long strides, restless energy prodding her steps. All her life she had devoted herself to hard work to attain whatever she had aspired to. Now she was faced with men who believed in a myth, and no amount of hard work was going to change their beliefs. She might fail at what she came to do because of something out of her control. She hated this helplessness assailing her.

She plowed her fingers into the thickness of her hair and held her head, rubbing her scalp, trying to relieve the tension throbbing behind her brow. Maybe the lush growth, the insects, the heat and humidity were all getting to her. Maybe the people, especially her father back in Dallas, were right. This wasn't a job for a woman who wasn't experienced in this type of field work, no matter how much the rain forest fascinated her, no matter how good a geologist she was.

Memories gnawed at her. She wanted to push them away, but they wouldn't leave her in peace. Hard work hadn't helped her prove herself to her father nor helped her marriage succeed. A tremor snaked down her spine, leaving in its wake an icy trail.

A sheen of tears glistened in her eyes as she stared at the lantern, reliving the feeling all over again that she had never been good enough for her father. Emotions she had tried to bury squeezed her heart painfully, forcing their way into her thoughts.

A lone tear coursed down her cheek. She never cried anymore and wasn't going to start now. She batted the tear away, sniffed and turned to pace again. With each step she took, her head pounded. Sitting in the hammock, she closed her eyes and kneaded her temples with her knuckles. Fatigue that she had held at bay embraced her. It clung to her, becoming a part of her.

"Can't sleep," she muttered, needing to open her eyes but hating to when the darkness was a balm to her throbbing head. A balm that would lure her into the blackness of sleep. A balm that would leave her at the mercy of her dreams—of *him*.

A picture of the man in her dreams flashed into her mind—tall, powerful, his body most likely conditioned by hard, physical labor. But it had been his eyes that intrigued her. Such an usual color, she thought, and knew it had to be a dream after all. She had never seen a man with eyes the color of burnished gold.

Hers snapped open. She had to stay awake. She retrieved the map and sat in the canvas chair by the lantern. In the golden glow she studied the map and tried to decide where they would go first when the rain stopped.

But as Kathleen surveyed the paper, the lines blurred and faded into gray blotches. She blinked. Her eyes were tired like the rest of her body. She laid the map in her lap, turned off the lantern and let her eyes drift closed for just a moment.

***

A cat's roar sliced through the rain-laden air, causing Kathleen to bolt to her feet. The map she held floated to the tarp. Another animal cry shuddered along her nerves. Alarmed, she whirled toward the tent flap, tension making her heart beat faster, her breathing quick shallow intakes. The curtain of black loomed before her in all its menacing possibilities, and for the life of her she couldn't get her heart to slow its rapid pace.

It was nightfall and it was still raining. She pushed back the tent flap. Outside, the blanket of ebony hung about her like the cape of a sinister vampire. Shivering from her fanciful thoughts, she fumbled for her lantern, turned it on and held it aloft, trying to penetrate the darkness to see where Santo and the others were. *Nothing*.

Oblivious to the drenching rain, she sloshed through several inches of water toward the area where Santo's tent was, the dim light from the lantern barely illuminating a foot in front of her. She found the tent and rushed inside. *Empty.*

Sweat broke out on her forehead, mingling with the rain to stream down her face. She tried to hold back the fear, to stay calm. But she couldn't as she scanned the tent. All signs of the men were gone. The only things left were the barren shell of canvas that sheltered her from the downpour and the jaguar skull on the pole sticking out of the water-saturated ground.

"Santo," she shouted, hoping he wasn't too far away.

Nothing but the sound of rain greeted her. Her gaze fastened upon the skull with its hollow eyes. *I'm alone.* That thought sank in as her feet sank into the water flowing through the tent.

She stared at the water rising about her and decided to head back to her tent which was situated on higher ground. Racing across the campsite, she reached the safety of her still dry tent, her clothes completely plastered against her skin. Even though the temperature was warm, she felt chilled. She wasn't sure if it was because her fear was growing or because it was getting colder and wetter.

She again sat in her chair and placed the lantern on the small table next to her. Why had Santo and his men left her alone? Maybe they were scouting the area out in case the place flooded. Maybe—

Who was she kidding? She knew they were gone. They had been panicked from the moment they had seen the jaguar and the skull. The man in the cave had scared them away as he had said he would. He was the reason she was sitting here in the rain, alone, frightened, and not sure how she would get out of the jungle alive.

She surveyed the dark edges of the night about her and realized she couldn't do anything until morning. Hopefully the rain would have stopped by then, and she could formulate a plan of action.

For the next several hours Kathleen listened to the rain batter the roof of her tent. She tried to keep her spirits up even as she watched the tarp become saturated with water. She couldn't allow panic to seep into her like the water into her tent. She had to remain calm and in control if she wanted to make it back to civilization. She kept herself busy by moving her supplies up off the ground, then by studying the map of the area to plan her escape.

Slowly the dim gray of dawn pressed back the black perimeter of night, and Kathleen could really assess how bad her situation was. She peered outside, and all she saw was water blanketing the whole rain forest floor. Even in her tent she stood in five or six inches of water. The fear she had tried to hold at bay seized her.

She had to get to the canoes. She prayed Santo had at least left her one of them. If he hadn't, she didn't care to think what would become of her. Quickly she stuffed her most important belongings into her backpack, slung it over her shoulder, and stepped out of her tent.

For a moment she stopped and turned around to make sure that Santo and his Indian helpers were truly gone. The tent they had shared was washed away, the canvas wrapped about a tree that bordered the campsite. Soon, if the rain continued, there would be no evidence she had even been here. Taking a deep, fortifying breath, she adjusted the yellow slicker's hood to cover her head better, then started forward.

The river was only a few hundred yards to the east. She pushed to the back of her mind the fact that all this water probably came from the river overflowing. She didn't have any choice. She had to try to make it to the site where Santo had stowed the canoes.

But as she went into the jungle, the water rose swiftly about the calves of her legs. As she trudged deeper into the dense green, it came up to her thighs, swirling about her. She squinted, trying to see through the mass of gray rain, trying to determine how deep the water was ahead of her.

Pushing debris out of her way, she continued forward. She had to be halfway there. Soon she would find the canoe Santo left for her and be safe. The current of water grew stronger with each step she took. A log struck her from behind and sent her to her knees. She tried to scramble to her feet, to keep her head from going under, but another piece of debris crashed into her. The blackness swirled before her like the water, sweeping her under and under.

***

He paced the cavern he called home, restless, frustrated, wanting—what? Coming to an abrupt halt, he swung around and looked at Kathleen. She lay on his bed, her eyes closed, her expression relaxed, for the moment at peace with the world. A peace he couldn't find, even in rest, he thought, and turned away from her tranquil image.

An energy, barely contained, rushed through him like the feeling he got when he was high in the trees, surveying the forest from the top. His life wasn't his anymore, had stopped being his five years before, the day his other life had come to an end. He belonged to the jungle now, as much a part of it as the plants, animals and insects that abounded in it.

Again he started pacing, his hands curling and uncurling at his sides. Her vision of fire intruded into his thoughts, drawing him back to her lying on his bed. She was dangerous for him. She lived in a world he had been forced to give up, and yet he couldn't get her out of his mind. She haunted him, stirring in him feelings that he could never allow to take root. He was afraid if they ever did they would twine about his heart until they choked the very life from him like a parasite sucking the essence from its host.

"Why didn't you leave when I warned you to?" he whispered to her still form.

He knew the answer even as he uttered the words. He hadn't really gone after her like the other intruders. He had gotten good at scaring people away from this area. And he had certainly never brought another soul to his home. Then why her? Why had he felt compelled to bring her to his cavern the night before last? He had known he wasn't going to change her mind about searching for the oil deposits. He had also known she wouldn't listen to his warning about the rain and the river flooding.

Plunging his fingers repeatedly through his hair, he tried to dismiss the real reason he hadn't been able to resist taking her from her campsite. He was drawn to her, and he realized the peril in that attraction. A warning from years past accentuated the danger of becoming involved. Dr. Kathleen Dawson was forbidden to him. He had no room for her in his life—a life she would never accept, a life he had dedicated himself to.

She stirred on his bed, moving her delicate hand up to her face to brush away her hair. He tensed. When her hand fell away and she settled back into a deep sleep, he moved to the bed and knelt beside it. An alarm went off in his mind and body, an alarm that always warned him of imminent danger, an alarm he always listened to—until now.

His fingers caressed her hair from her face, her skin soft beneath his stroke. A tightness in his gut tautened into a twisting knot as his hand lingered on her cheek for a brief moment, then followed the curve of her jawline to the hollow at the base of her throat.

The beat of her pulse flowed from her and into him. He squeezed his eyes shut and felt her life forces flood him with her feminine nature. His mind touched hers, and he sensed her vulnerability, her determination and her deep sadness. His hand trembled as he snatched it away from her and shot to his feet. He didn't want nor understand this connection, but he couldn't seem to turn away from it.

"Damn!" he whispered to the silent walls of his cave, now his prison, trapped with her until the waters receded.

He had to check and make sure the Xango Indians were all right, that the flooding hadn't affected them. Dawn would be breaking over the treetops soon. He didn't want to leave her, but he had no other choice. He had lost the chance to choose his own destiny. Quickly he strode toward the passageway that she had taken in her flight to escape him an eternity ago.

                              ***

When Kathleen woke up, she knew she was back in the cave. She felt the soft leaves beneath her, smelled the damp muskiness of the cavern, and heard water dripping from the limestone. She lay for a moment, trying to decide what to do. Her head ached where the log had hit her. Her body was sore. Her mouth was as dry as she wished the forest were.

He had rescued her, a man whose name she didn't even know. A man who had intentionally frightened her guide and his helpers away. Feelings, all confused and tangled up in desire she didn't want to feel, swirled about inside her.

Slowly she opened her eyes halfway and looked about her. At first she thought the cave was empty and couldn't help feeling disappointed. Then she saw it and fear struck her.

The jaguar sat by the dying fire as though it had not a care in the world. Thoughts ceased as Kathleen stared into the yellow eyes of death, only feet from her, gleaming from an inner light that sent chills down her spine.

Slowly at first, then rapidly as the jaguar stood, she began to think. *I should have left when he insisted two days ago.* Her heart leaped into her throat, clogging it. *Now it's too late.*

Frantically she sat up, and the pain that tapped a throbbing rhythm against her skull intensified. Darting a glance about her, she searched for a means of escape. But she was trapped. She knew the passageway was a stone maze that offered her no hope, but she couldn't remain here waiting for the cat to make its move. Her fingers clenched a fist full of leaves so tightly her hand ached. While she chewed on her lower lip, she tried to decide how she was going to make it to that passageway without alarming the jaguar.

She slowly rose inch by inch.

The black cat emitted a roar that jolted her heart into a maddening flutter, heightening her sense of danger until she felt her legs shaking so much that she went to her knees. He leisurely advanced toward her. Panic held her immobile.

Oh, my God, this is it. He knows I can't escape, and he's taking his time, toying with me.

Her heart stopped beating, her breathing captured in her lungs, burning, constricting. She tried to stand, to flee, but every muscle refused to function, as if her body knew the uselessness of running while her mind demanded she do something—anything.

The jaguar came to a halt a step from her and sat on his haunches, his yellow eyes glowing in the blackness of his face. The pressure in her chest screamed for her to breathe. She dragged air into her lungs, short, shallow gasps that hissed in the eerie silence, the sound echoing in her mind as if it were a death knell.

His yellow gaze bore into her with a vehemence that unnerved her, and yet suddenly she sensed the cat wouldn't hurt her. Was it wishful thinking? The throbbing in her head hammered a message of caution against her temples.

Minutes crawled by as they stared at each other, eye to eye. She had to do something. They couldn't stay like this forever. A meowing purr erupted in the stillness, then the cat came to its feet and walked away from her.

Kathleen started to crumple to the ground but caught herself. Watching the cat stalk the large cavern, surveying the area, she struggled to her feet, her gaze fastened onto his sleek body, moving in a graceful flow that she couldn't help admiring. His sensuous lines, his rich ebony fur magnified her appreciation.

The jaguar stopped by the now cold fire and stretched out on the ground, his head resting between his front paws, his gaze seeking hers, watching her. Stunned, Kathleen retreated until the stone wall caressed her back.

What am I supposed to do now? Where is my rescuer? Why isn't he here?

Question after question swept through her mind, not to stay long in the turbulent confusion that possessed her.

The pounding against her temples escalated even more. Closing her eyes, she shut out the world and went through a mental relaxation technique she often used. It didn't work. Her body was so wound up every muscle ached from tension.

She came to a decision. She had to know the cat's intentions.

On shaky legs she approached the jaguar. It was her turn to come to a halt in front of the big cat. He continued to lie on the ground as if oblivious to her approach.

Squatting down in front of him, she started to touch his fur. A shudder rippled down her body. She buried her fingernails into the soft flesh of her palms, crossing her arms over her chest in a protective gesture.

You're safe with me.

The alien thought invaded her mind. Shocked, she felt the trembling start in her hands and quickly spread throughout her body. Even though she was shaking, the calming thought continued to weave its way through her head, bringing with it a serenity she hadn't believed possible.

Touch me.

His gentle command compelled her to obey. Gradually she unfurled her fingers and moved her hand toward the jaguar. It seemed like an eternity before she felt the softness of the black pelt beneath her palm. Her fingers tingled as she tunneled them into the rich fur. The chill that had permeated her vanished as the warmth from the cat invaded her body like his silent reassurance had her mind.

"Why are you here?" she asked, not really expecting an answer and surprised when she heard the words, *I'm here for you*, in her mind.

The jaguar allowed her to caress his fur for a few minutes longer, the sound of his contentment purring from his throat. Then all of a sudden he leaped to his feet, his head angled as though he was listening to something.

Kathleen strained to hear what had alarmed him, but all she heard was the thundering of her own heartbeat. The jaguar raced toward the passageway and disappeared.

Minutes crawled by, leaving Kathleen to wonder what had happened to the jaguar and to the man who was both her tormentor and her savior.

He appeared out of the darkness like a long-ago warrior. His machete was strapped to his waist. Dangerous looking. Magnificent in a primitively masculine way. And he was the reason she had been left alone.

Anger shoved caution into the background as she watched him approach her, his gaze scanning the cave, ever alert, wary. She drew herself up straight and met his look with one full of fury.

"Are you satisfied? You managed to scare away my Indian guides, leaving me alone."

"I hadn't intended for them to leave without you."

"But they did, and I almost drowned because of you." Her hands knotted into fists.

"But you didn't. You're safe."

She arched a brow. "I am?"

He didn't say anything.

"There was a jaguar here a few minutes ago. I could have been mauled by the animal." Her voice rose with each word she spoke while she advanced the few feet to him.

"I know."

"You do?"

"There is little I don't know about in my territory. You were safe." He looked away then back at her. "He's a friend."

"Like the monkey the other night?" She remembered feeling as though she had stepped into the middle of a Tarzan movie.

"Not exactly. The monkey is Zenna's pet, and sometimes he wanders down here. The jaguar was guarding you for me until I could return. Jaguars aren't man-eaters, and they are rarely aggressive."

The predatory ring to his words sent a shiver down her spine. "Since it was your tricks that scared the Indians away, you damn well should feel responsibility for this situation. What are you going to do about it?"

"Nothing."

"Nothing!" she said in a seething voice. "Doing nothing is a sure way to get rid of your problem. I see you were just going to leave me in my camp to find my own way out of the jungle or die. I guess I should feel grateful you decided to rescue me from drowning. Why didn't you just let me die? All your problems would be gone just like that." She snapped her fingers in front of his face.

Anger overwhelmed her. She raised her fists and pounded them against his naked chest. Tears welled up into her throat, choking off any more words. She didn't want to cry, didn't want to give him the satisfaction of seeing her tears, but they flowed from her eyes as she hammered her frustration and fury into him.

Finally when she had no energy left even to raise her hands, she backed away a few steps, desperately trying to control the tears that continued to course down her cheeks. Ever since her father had chosen his work over her graduation, she had not cried. Sniffling, she inhaled deep gulps of air, upset that this man made her lose control. How could he in such a short time provoke her to tears? What was happening to her?

"Are you through?" he asked, his own anger threading through his words.

"Yes, I would say I'm through. You've seen to that."

The fight was gone from her voice. Instead, she struggled to retain enough determination to remain standing, but her mind spun with her confusion and conflicting emotions. Lightheaded, she swayed. He was instantly by her side, picking her up into his strong arms and carrying her toward his bed.

His arms surrounding her gave her comfort when she should have been fighting their cage. His gaze that probed her face conveyed a peace she shouldn't have felt. His scent wove its way through her body. Exhausted, she laid her head against his chest and listened to his heart pulsing beneath her ear. The sound was like the beat of a drum, pounding out a sensuous dance that they alone moved to.

Alarmed at how easy it was for him to influence her, she lifted her head, growing taut in his embrace. "Put me down. Now."

"In a second." He placed her on the soft leaves, then straightened, towering above her like a conquering warrior, a smug expression evident on his face.

Her anger reasserted itself as she scrambled to sit up and push him away with her feet. He seized her legs, laughter rumbling from his chest.

"I can see that you're okay," he said, amusement heavy in his voice.

"Do you give a damn?"

The grin that teased the edges of his mouth vanished. "That's the problem. I do."

"You call leaving me alone to fend for myself giving a damn?"

"As I said, I was watching. I wouldn't have let anything happen to you."

"What happened to the Indians? Where are they?"

He shrugged. "I suspect by now they are home in the capital with their families."

"I can't believe they left me alone. I'm alone." As she said those last two words, her situation fully sank into her. This man was her only means of getting out of the jungle in one piece. She'd never been good with directions and had no idea which way to go.

He pinned her with a look that quivered down the length of her to the tips of her toes. "You aren't alone. I'm here."

"And that's supposed to make me feel better? You're the reason the Indians left in the first place. You, and that jaguar myth."

"And you have turned my world upside down. Whether I like it or not, you are my responsibility now."

Frowning, he began to prowl the domains of his home, much like the jaguar had. She watched him, feeling the caged energy trapped inside him. It was an almost palpable force that encompassed the area about him, a force she was beginning to wonder if he could contain.

Two nights before when they had touched, she had felt his emotions, so strong at times they were overpowering. For the past few days things that she would have thought impossible before were becoming her reality—a reality she couldn't control nor define but was wrapped up in this man before her.

Could he really be the mythical Jaguar Man? She stared at him as he continued to stalk the cavern.

Swinging her legs to the dirt floor, she stood and covered the distance between them. "Are you real? Or, am I really going crazy? Which is it?" She reached out and touched him, snapping her hand back after the briefest of connections. She still felt the tingling sensation in the tips of her fingers. It seemed very real to her. She also felt something else—his loneliness, his sadness? Looking into his neutral expression, she rejected the idea that she could sense his feelings from a brief touch. Was it another impossibility she was finding was possible?

He smiled, a faint lifting of the corners of his mouth, but the gesture gleamed in his eyes. "Go ahead. *Really* touch me. This time I want you to be sure, Kathleen. I'm not something you've dreamed. You won't wake up tomorrow in camp."

The challenge was a hypnotic dare that lured her closer, as if she were Eve in the Garden of Eden and he were the Serpent, bent on enticing her against all she believed in. She took half a step nearer until she could breathe in his scent of jungle and man. With a shaky hand she laid her fingers on his bare arm, the feel beneath her skin warm and rough. She slid her hand up his arm, reveling in the rugged texture and sinew under her palm. Emotions poured into her, his emotions blending with hers. She needed to break contact but couldn't. She was discovering that to touch him was like a sweet obsession she didn't want to give up.

He arched a brow. "Well, am I real enough for you? I thought we had this straight."

She made the mistake of looking up at that moment and being ensnared in the golden depths of his eyes. Rich, like the precious metal she thought of when she looked into them. Warm, like the sun on the treetops. Intense, like the atmosphere sizzling between them. Words vaporized in her thoughts as her gaze delved beneath the depths, seeking answers she felt he kept secreted away from the world. For some unknown reason she was privy to them, as though he couldn't keep his guard up around her.

"I don't understand what's going on. I've never had trouble making up my mind before. When I'm with you, you seem real. When I'm not, you're like a dream, a phantom of the night."

Again she felt his emotions caress her soul, felt his desire hot in her blood, heating her up. Stunned, she broke away, first visually then physically, and put the space of the cavern between them. But even from across the room, she still felt connected emotionally, and that realization was disconcerting. She worked hard to keep her feelings hidden, often even from herself, because to feel was to open herself up to rejection. And she had had more than her share of rejections.

Turning about, trying to divert her thoughts away from him, she tapped the top of the trunk along the rock wall and started to lift up the lid. "Will I find answers to your secrets in here?"

He moved so fast, so silently, she was taken completely by surprise. He closed his large hand about her arm and twisted her around to face him, the sound of the lid slamming shut reverberating through the cavern.

His fierce expression robbed her of her next breath.

Chapter Three

"What's in there you don't want me to see?" Kathleen asked, feeling the sudden change in the atmosphere as though a storm were about to erupt.

"Secrets best left unknown."

The menacing threat in his voice unnerved her more than anything else that had happened to her since her first encounter with him. His anger swamped her and, for a few seconds, obliterated any other feelings inside her.

Fear clogged her throat, making words of protest at his painful grip impossible to utter. Swallowing several times, she finally managed to reassert herself, to force his emotions away. "You're hurting me."

The glazed anger in his eyes evaporated. His clasp on her eased, but he still held her as if afraid she would tempt the fates and open his Pandora's box. "Promise me you won't touch this trunk again."

She nodded, too afraid to do anything but that. He stared at her for a long moment. Seemingly satisfied by her response, he backed away. She finally took a deep, cleansing breath to still her frantic heartbeat. But the old trunk continued to lure her as though it called out to her to open it. She clasped her hands tightly in front of her and looked away, acknowledging the danger in pursuing the answers to the mysteries shrouding this man.

As he paced the cavern, Kathleen sat on the edge of the bed, searching for a topic of conversation to break the tension-fraught silence between them. "What is your name? I can't be referring to you as the man in the cave."

He chuckled, the sound relieving the tension of moments before, diffusing the strong emotions flying between them. "At least I'm fortunate you haven't used more descriptive words than that."

"Somehow if I had, I think it wouldn't have bothered you."

His laughter reverberated from the walls of the cave, sending heated sensations flowing over her. He wasn't supposed to make her feel, but she did. She was all too aware of his masculine qualities, which appealed to her on a passionate, primitive level. She couldn't help wondering at the emotional connection between them. When they touched, she felt things within him that shouldn't be possible. She had never been psychic before.

"True, Kathleen. Long ago I stopped worrying about what others thought."

For a brief moment she felt transported to another place, another time, striving to do her best, sacrificing her wishes and desires to do what others thought she should. She realized she had lived her life for others, doing what was expected of her, even to the point of becoming a geologist to be closer to her father. She had always thought that if they shared a career they would share other things as well. She was wrong. He didn't think she could do the job, in fact had insisted she not come to Costa Sierra, saying she wasn't equipped to deal with the primitive environment of the jungle. That had made this trip all the more important to her, even to the extent that she had come ahead of the others.

"What should I call you?" she asked, refusing to think about that last meeting with her father.

"Some of the natives call me Guerriro."

"Warrior? Why?" When her gaze skimmed over him, she had to acknowledge he looked every inch a warrior—massive, powerful, dangerous.

"I fight for them."

"Guerriro," she said, testing the word on her lips. "I suppose it's better than the man in the cave, but why are you afraid to tell me your real name?"

"The name I was born with?"

She nodded.

"I'm not that man anymore. He's dead."

"Why do you say that? What happened to that man?"

He glanced beyond her toward the trunk, and just for a second, she saw a bleak look in his eyes before he managed to mask the emotion.

"What happened?" Kathleen persisted, suddenly sure the explanation was important.

"The jungle has a way of swallowing up a person—changing that person."

"Is that trunk where you keep all your tricks to convince the Indians you're some kind of Jaguar Man?"

Kneeling, he returned his attention to the fire, stoking it, building it higher with pieces of wood he had nearby.

"Are you the Jaguar Man?" She neared him, ignoring the threat conveyed in the straightening of his spine, the flexing of his hands.

He whipped his head around to trap her with his discerning gaze. "I thought you didn't believe in the legend."

"I don't. They do."

"Do I look like a Jaguar Man?" He rose to stand with his feet planted apart, his hands on his hips, everything in his stance transmitting a proud countenance—like a warrior.

She tried to appear as though she was objectively studying him as she would a rock specimen. But while her gaze brushed over his muscular chest and down toward his flat stomach, she lost all objectivity. The man part in the name was correct, no doubt about it, she thought, as she strived unsuccessfully to still the racing of her pulse.

When the silence had become embarrassingly long, she finally reestablished eye contact with him. "I don't know. I've never seen a Jaguar Man. If the legend is to be believed, the person is a man by night and a jaguar by day."

"But you don't believe the legend?"

"I'm a scientist. I work with facts, not rumors. Transformation is not scientifically possible."

"Not everything can be explained away rationally. There are mysteries in this world."

"Oh, so you're telling me you are the Jaguar Man, and that you can change form? Show me," she demanded, all her doubt apparent in her tone of voice.

Guerriro laughed, lifting his hand to brush her hair away from her face. She should have moved back, but her legs refused her brain's command. She stood in front of him as though entranced. His hands rested heavily on her shoulders, his thumbs massaging hot circles into her flesh. She wanted to melt into him.

"Ah, Kathleen, that would be a neat trick, changing into a jaguar, but I'm afraid I'll have to disappoint you."

"Just as I suspected. I don't believe in the legend, and I don't believe in fairy tales either."

"So you don't think there is such a thing as a happily ever after for two people?"

"Not from what I've seen of relationships." First her mother and father's marriage and then her own.

"And what have you seen?" he asked, his voice a husky whisper that enveloped her in visions of happily ever afters.

She wished his hands would stop their sensuous kneading. She felt as if her bones would melt into a pool of liquid at his feet. Her eyes drifted closed for a few seconds as she tried to compose an answer that would make sense, as she fought the desire seeping from him into her, becoming an intricate part of her, much like the air she breathed.

"What has made you so unhappy?" His hands traveled up her neck to frame her face. By tilting her head up, he forced her to look at him, his eyes a molten brand.

"Nothing," was all she could manage to choke out as he leaned nearer until his breath fused with hers.

"That's not true, Kathleen. I can feel it deep inside you. It eats away at your soul."

Again their emotions blended as though they were one. She wanted to deny the link; she couldn't this time.

His palms felt like hot coals upon her cheeks, his scent like the mist in early morning, rising up from the ground to swallow her in gray swirls. He buried his hands in her hair while his gaze touched the pulse-beat at her throat before slowly trekking upward to her slightly parted lips, then continuing onward to her eyes. The electric shock of his regard flashed down her body, making her every cell aware of him only inches away. Gone were the feelings from the past; now all that mattered was this man who held her captive in every sense.

He bent even nearer, until his lips were a whisper away, his eyes sliding closed for a few seconds. A tremor passed through his body into hers, and her throat tightened about each breath she inhaled. Again he shuddered as though fighting with himself.

His eyes bolted open, his hands dropping away. He stepped back. "This isn't a fairy tale or a legend This is real. As soon as the river recedes and it's safe, I want you to leave this rain forest."

A heated blush tinted her cheeks. Kathleen felt robbed and hated the anticipation he had created in her, then shattered with such ease. He had fought his desire and won. She grasped onto an emotion she could control—anger—and directed it at him.

"No, you want me. I can feel your desire and you're afraid of that."

He turned away from her and put more wood on the fire. "I don't want to force you from the jungle, but I will if I have no other choice. My wants are unimportant. My only concern is the Indians who live here."

Chills caused from the lethal quiet of his voice rose on her skin. "Give me one good reason why I should turn my back on all I've worked for."

"Me."

That one word froze the blood in her body. "What can I do that will be so harmful?"

"You fool! I told you it isn't you but the people who will follow. They can't come into this jungle and leave it untouched."

"If this oil deposit is as big as I think it is, the world needs it. Oil is a finite resource that at the moment the world depends on, whether you or I like it. That's a fact."

"I see you and I don't agree, which leaves me very little choice in the matter."

"What do you mean?"

Ignoring her question, he knelt again by the fire.

She watched him calmly place yet another stick on the fire as if the cave were cold when in actuality she was hot. "Answer me!" Panic laced her words.

"Kathleen, you and I are confined here until it stops raining and the river recedes. Then I'll see that you leave."

In that moment she had a strong urge to pummel his back with her fists, but she knew the effect would be futile. Instead, she pivoted away and stalked to the bed, putting space between them.

She drew in a deep breath, then released it slowly. Nothing alleviated the burning sensation in her lungs; she couldn't seem to get a decent breath. She was going crazy and falling apart at the same time. Under normal circumstances she would never have allowed herself to feel such intense emotions about a person, especially a stranger. But these weren't normal circumstances. Ever since she entered the rain forest, she had been aware of stepping into an alien environment, a part of herself shedding as though she were the one transforming.

"I won't leave until I have finished what I came to do."

"Work is very important to you."

"Of course. I've worked long and hard to get where I am. I have years of schooling, took jobs I didn't like, had to fight my way up through the company. But then I don't expect you to identify with that."

An amused expression fleetingly possessed his features. "Why not?"

"I only have to take one look around me to come to that conclusion."

"So you do all that hard work for the money?"

She frowned. "No, I have other reasons."

"What are they?"

There was no way she was going to tell Guerriro about her desire to make a difference in the world, about her need to be accepted by her father, about the failed marriage which had left her feeling insecure, floundering for a purpose, an identity. "How long have you lived here?" she asked instead.

He faced her. "An eternity," he finally said after several minutes.

"How many years?" she shot back, wanting to know as much as she could about this stranger who had put her at risk then saved her.

"Why is your search for oil so important to you? It's more than your job."

She ignored his probing question, not wanting to give of herself anymore than she had already. "How many years, Guerriro?" Every moment she was in his presence she felt herself slipping away.

He speared her with his intense eyes. "Five." The harsh lines of his face deepened, casting his rugged countenance into a sinister expression. "Why search for oil here? There are other places. There are even other places in Costa Sierra."

Kathleen knew she should be afraid, that all common sense in her demanded she be. But she wasn't. "You never answered me before. Are you the one responsible for the legend of the Jaguar Man?" She rose.

His gaze sliced into her and everything around her seemed to stop, all sounds, all movements. The dryness in her throat returned.

"Are you?" she pressed him, suddenly needing the confirmation of her suspicions.

"Yes."

"You use their superstitious fear to your advantage." This time she turned away in disgust. Her ex-husband had used her need for approval to his advantage, until she had felt her life was not hers anymore. She had fought hard to regain control of her life and swore after her divorce that she would never give it over to another person again.

"I do use the Indians' superstitious nature to protect their home and their lives."

"Is that what you call scaring them until they're afraid to walk in a part of the jungle you have deemed off limits? Who the hell do you think you are, playing with people's lives like you do?"

"And you don't think you play with their lives when you bring in outsiders to give them illnesses they have no immunity to, to change their way of life because it's the *civilized* thing to do?"

He advanced toward her, his anger communicated in an icy calm tone which was more threatening than if he had declared he intended her harm. Her eyes widened. She backed up against the wall and felt her vulnerability in every fiber of her being. He halted a foot in front of her, his eyes glowing like liquified gold, hot, blistering.

Her throat contracted, and she tried to work its muscles to speak.

He moved even closer, and she was trapped against the wall and him, both solid, unyielding. "It's obvious you don't believe that your presence will change their lives. I can see that nothing I say will change your mind. I'll just have to show you it will."

"How?" she croaked out, the constriction in her throat easing a little.

"In my own time, my own way."

He touched her hair, taking a strand and curling it around his finger. "My sole duty is to the people who live here. Outsiders are not welcome."

The softness in his voice belied the threat in his words. Kathleen no longer felt trapped by a physical means but by an emotional one. He took her head within his large hands, molding his fingers to her scalp, and closed his eyes.

She succumbed to the silence, to his touch. She wanted to suppress the feelings his nearness produced in her, but her body reacted on its own. Her chest tensed about each breath, her heart raced with anticipation. Her desire mingled with his like the merging of two adjoining rivers to become one.

"You don't fear me now, do you, Kathleen?" His eyes opened slowly.

The muscles in her body seemed to melt at the gently spoken question. She clasped onto his arms to steady herself while her gaze clasped his and became lost in its hot intensity.

"No," she murmured, licking her dry lips in a nervous gesture she knew was sending the wrong signal to him, but she didn't care.

With his hands still framing her face, he said, "I feel your desire, Kathleen. Do you feel mine?"

A small gasp escaped her lips. She felt as though he was reaching into her mind and becoming part of her. That insight stunned her, frightened her, because she let no one get close to her. And she couldn't control this uniting of emotions, of souls, that went beyond anything she had ever experienced.

Kathleen's hold on him tightened, her fingertips turning white. One of his hands slipped lower and came to rest over her heart. With his other hand he placed her splayed fingers over his heart. Its rapid, rhythmic beat matched hers, rushing into her, filling her with his desire.

"They beat as if one," he whispered, the declaration binding her to him as if their hearts were truly united.

"I don't understand what is happening to me. Why do I feel what you feel?"

He grinned, a lopsided lifting of one corner of his mouth. "Neither do I. For all sane purposes I should never have brought you here that first night."

"Then why did you?" The inquiry came out breathless, barely audible.

But he heard and smiled. "That's a good question."

"But one you aren't going to answer?"

He buried his hands in the long strands of her hair and looked into her eyes. "No."

"What do you want from me? And don't tell me it's that you want me to leave the jungle. That's not why you brought me here that first night."

Before Kathleen could react, he crushed his mouth into hers, holding her head still while the grinding pressure of his lips demanded her response. She wanted to push him away, to scrub away his touch because she felt her very nature slipping from her with each second his kiss claimed her. And yet, she wanted to dissolve into his toughened contours, to return his ardent brand with one of her own.

Her body took the decision away from her mind. Her arms came up to encircle him, drawing him even closer as his mouth softened its assault to a passionate joining that did more to frighten her than his hard possession of seconds before. But no matter how much the rational side of her wanted to fight this attraction, she found herself welcoming the invasion of his tongue parting her lips to delve inside, the feel of his rough hands roaming over her back in a feverish search. She gloried in the sensations bursting outward from her feminine core to absorb any doubts.

While he took possession of her mouth, he unbuttoned her grungy white shirt and parted the material to unclasp her bra. His touch excited her as he cupped her breast, playing with the nipple, its peak tautening. She was his. That was telegraphed to him as her hands frantically traveled over the planes of his chest, exploring its muscled expanse with a womanly appreciation.

Breaking the kiss, his mouth a breath away, he sighed and touched his forehead to hers for a moment before he leaned back. "Does that answer your question? You were right. I want you, Kathleen. And I can't have you." He pushed away from her, a visible struggle for control taking place within him.

She almost asked why, then realized what she was doing. She wanted him, too, a stranger who was playing mind games with her. This yearning for him was eroding everything she had painstakingly built up over the years. Struggling for control of her emotions, she resolved not to give in to this weakness.

He walked to the table, poured two drinks, and handed her a cup.

"Is this the potion you gave me the other night?" she asked with suspicion.

"No. This is a herbal brew that has a calming effect." He downed his drink in two swallows.

"What is going to happen? How long will I need to stay here?"

He turned away, one of his hands combing through his midnight dark hair while the other still grasped the empty cup. "You'll stay until it's safe for you to go back."

The loneliness in his voice tore at her heart, compressing her lungs as though someone were squeezing the last bit of air from them. She fought the desire to reach out to him. She *knew* he would reject her touch, and she also knew that she wouldn't be able to handle his rejection.

He swung around and sat on the log by the fire. "Sit. Relax. Enjoy the drink."

All trace of loneliness was gone, and in its place was a forced cheerfulness. She did as he asked, sitting on the bed and taking several sips of the herbal drink. "Mmm. This is delicious. But then I thought the other potion was, too."

"Tell me about yourself, Kathleen."

"I work for Dalco Oil Company. I have a doctorate in geology."

"Only bare facts that I already knew. Tell me details."

"My work is my life."

"No man in your life?"

"No."

"Never?"

She looked away from Guerriro's penetrating gaze. "I was married once while in college. It only lasted a few years." Long, miserable years, she added silently, not ready to share the pain of her past marriage because she had never been able to. "Okay, now that I have told you something about myself, it's your turn."

He grinned. "Tit for tat?"

"You got it. Not another word about me until you share something with me."

"More drink." He held up the wooden pitcher, humor deep in his eyes.

"Something other than food or drink."

"I believe I already told you I was the one responsible for the Jaguar Man myth. Doesn't that count?"

"What made you come up with a legend about a man-jaguar? Why did you go to all that trouble? How did you come to the rain forest in the first place?"

"Whoa. I'll answer your last question. Like you I came to the jungle to plunder."

"Then why—"

He shook his head. "That's all you'll get from me, Kathleen. Now, one of my questions. Who or what are you running away from?"

Shocked at his perception, she stood. That was something else she wasn't prepared to discuss. It would make their relationship even more personal, intimate. She was desperately trying to keep it as impersonal as possible, which she was beginning to think was unlikely. "I think this exchange is one-sided."

"You will tell me one of these days, Kathleen."

"You make all this sound long term. Once the rain stops and the river recedes, I plan on searching for the oil. I didn't come all this way to go back empty handed."

His chuckle filled the cavern. "Plans can change, Kathleen. How are you going to search for the oil?"

"Are you going to keep me here? I thought you said I could leave once the rain stops."

Chapter Four

"I won't keep you here. No one wants you to leave more than I do."

Kathleen wished Guerriro's words didn't hurt, but they did. That realization stunned her because his world was thousands of miles from hers. She was fascinated by the rain forest but never in her wildest dreams could she picture herself living here as he did. After she obtained her goal, she wanted to leave, too.

"But I can't let you continue your search."

His declaration knotted her stomach into a tight ball. She walked to where he was sitting by the fire and thrust her cup out in front of her. "I could use some more." After he had poured her more herbal brew, she took a long swallow and asked, "Do you think I will calmly let you dictate to me what I am going to do and not do?"

"No. I believe I will have my hands full convincing you that it's in everyone's best interest to leave this place undisturbed."

"It won't be in my best interest or in Dalco's."

He rose, towering over her. "I'll just have to change your best interest."

One part of her wanted to back away from the power emanating from him. The other part held her rooted to the spot only inches from him.

"I can be very stubborn." She lifted her chin a notch as though to emphasize her words while inside she quivered with doubt that she could win any battle with this man.

"Ah, your tough facade. You forget that I can feel what is beneath it."

She blinked, breaking visual contact with him. Again she saw the trunk against the stone wall and knew answers were underneath its lid. She was drawn to it but realized the folly in that lure. Bringing her hands up to her forehead, she massaged her temples as if that would chase away the dull ache behind her eyes.

Guerriro laid his hand on her shoulder, and she jerked away, startled by the jolt of feelings arcing between them in that brief tactile connection. "You're tired. You need to rest."

She backed away several feet, shaking her head, wishing she could deny the union she felt between him that went beyond the physical. She was a woman of science and yet everything that had occurred to her since meeting Guerriro went against her beliefs. "What's happening here? I've been all over the world and met countless people. This has never happened to me before. It's as if I know you on a level I've never before experienced." She continued to shake her head as though that would refute her statement. "Have you done something to me? Is that concoction you gave me doing this?"

"Do you think I want to feel your emotions?" he thundered, the sound reverberating off the stone walls. "I thought I had given all that up years ago."

"Given what up?"

He pivoted away from her and strode toward the passageway. "Get some rest."

Then he was gone, leaving her alone with her unanswered questions. She started after him, but immediately thought

better of it. She remembered all too vividly the other night and
her disastrous escape attempt. She recalled being totally lost in
the stone maze surrounding the cavern. A shudder of fear and
vulnerability racked her. Even though there were no bars
around her, she felt like a prisoner, shackled by his threats, by
the dark unknown that lay beyond his lair.

Kathleen slowly turned full circle, her gaze coming to rest
on the trunk. She walked to it and placed her hand on its lid.
Indecision warred within her. He had extracted a promise from
her that she wasn't sure she could keep. If she couldn't get
some answers soon from him, she knew her natural curiosity
would lead her to do something she might regret. She snatched
her hand away and held it up in front of her , feeling as though
contact with the trunk had burned her. She trembled at the
thought of what Guerriro would do to her if he discovered her
going through his possessions.

Suddenly the tension of the past few days drenched her in
exhaustion, and she felt as if the weight of the stone cavern
rested on her shoulders. She moved to sit on the bed of leaves.
The throbbing in her head intensified. She closed her eyes and
lay down to rest. Not because he said so, but because her body
demanded it. But when she was fully herself again, she would
discover the answers she needed and find a way to continue
what she had come to do. No one—not even a person
responsible for a myth—was going to deter her from her path.
She was determined to prove to her father that she was as
capable as any man. Then maybe the demons that had hounded
her all these years would be silent.

***

When Kathleen awakened, she found the black jaguar
lying by the fire. Its yellow eyes bore into her with astonishing
intensity. She remembered that same look from Guerriro and
shivered. It wasn't possible for a man to become a jaguar. She
knew that as a scientist, but on a primeval level she had her
doubts. What if he were the—

She clasped her head as if that action would still the disquieting thoughts. The laws of science applied here. She had not landed in an alien world, even though there were times she felt she had. Drawing in several deep breaths, she calmly swung her legs over the edge of the bed.

When she rose, her knees nearly buckled. She grasped the platform and steadied herself. Willing strength into her limbs, she covered the distance to the fire and the jaguar. She squatted down next to the animal and started to reach forward to pet him. She froze.

What was she thinking? This wasn't a house cat. This animal was a hunter, a fierce predator. He staked his territory and patrolled it, protecting it. Again she thought of Guerriro and his role in the rain forest.

I would like you to touch me. The thought came unbidden into her mind. She shot to her feet, again shaken by the silent intrusion.

I will not hurt you.

Kathleen took a step back, transfixed by the yellow gleam in the jaguar's eyes. She was definitely going crazy. There was no other explanation that made sense to her. Animals did not transmit their thoughts to humans. Period.

She turned away and hurried back to the bed of leaves. Sitting on the platform, she brought her legs up to her chest and clasped them to her. With her chin resting on her knees, she stared at the big cat; he stared at her. Her heart pumped the blood through her body at a maddening pace. She could hear it pound in her ears like the roar of a waterfall.

Did she want to feel safe so much that she imagined the jaguar was harmless? Guerriro had said the cat was his pet, a friend. Even if that was so, that didn't mean the jaguar was her friend. She glanced about the cavern. Being a woman of action, she knew she couldn't spend her time cornered on the platform, afraid to move. The last time the jaguar hadn't done anything to her. Maybe if she acted as if he wasn't here, everything would be all right.

Carefully she stood on unsteady legs and cautiously walked to the other side of the fire where a bowl of food sat on the table. Hunger pains contracted her stomach, and she reached out to grab a piece of a strange looking fruit. She didn't know where Guerriro was, but surely he was going to feed her. She took a bite of the fruit and savored its sweet taste. That was all the encouragement she needed. She delved into the rest of the food.

When she had satisfied her hunger, she again surveyed the cavern, assessing her prison of stone. There was little of interest except the trunk. She remembered Guerriro's warning not to look inside. Placing the wooden bowl down on the roughly hewn table, she moved toward the forbidden.

Out of the corner of her eye she caught a flash of black. The jaguar jumped to his feet and with a graceful leap, landed between her and the trunk. He sat on his haunches and stared at her, a menacing guard separating her and Guerriro's Pandora's box. A low purr rumbled from the cat, issuing his own warning to her to go no farther.

"Okay, I won't," she said and turned away.

Where was Guerriro? What in the world was she to do with herself? She would go crazy for sure if she couldn't find something to do with her time. She liked to keep busy. She didn't want to have to stop and be forced to think about her past, about her future—about her present.

She began to prowl the cavern, her gaze darting to the passageway every few seconds. The jaguar stretched out in front of the trunk which she made sure she avoided in her trek about her stone prison. She counted her steps from one side to the other, then walked off the width of the cave, calculating its dimensions to be one hundred feet by seventy.

By her watch she knew an hour had passed, and yet to her it seemed like half a day. She felt as though she were crawling out of her skin. She wouldn't last if she didn't find something to occupy her time and her overactive imagination.

Suddenly the atmosphere in the cave changed. She knew she wasn't alone. The jaguar rolled to his feet and sauntered forward. Kathleen came to a halt and whirled about, expecting to see Guerriro in the passageway. She gasped at the sight of a short man with weathered skin, bronzed by the sun, his body nearly naked except for the loincloth he wore. Ear plugs with long feathers dangled from his lobes, and his face and chest were scored with geometric designs in black and red paint. His short black hair was streaked with gray and very even, as though he had placed a bowl on top of his head to indicate where to cut. With a spear in one hand, a torch in his other, and a large bow and quiver of arrows slung across his back, he was the very picture of an Indian warrior on the hunt.

Speechless, she remained in the middle of the cavern, unable to move, unable to scream, unable to think.

"I have come for you," the Indian said in Spanish.

She thought of the stories of headhunters and wondered if any shrunken heads adorned his hut. "You have?" she murmured, suddenly aware of the jaguar nudging her hand, the feel of his fur soft, luxurious beneath her fingers, prompting a calmness to descend when she should be afraid of this new stranger.

"Come." The elderly man motioned for her to follow him into the dark passageway.

If the jaguar hadn't brushed up against her, she wouldn't have moved. She felt as if the black cat was prodding her toward the Indian. Nearing the man, she felt some more of her tension melt at the friendly look in his chocolate brown eyes. He smiled, displaying several missing teeth.

"Come before it begins to rain again."

"It has stopped?"

"For now."

Hope blossomed. She would be able to leave sooner than she had thought. She passed him in the corridor, the light from his torch showing her the way forward. "Are you taking me to the capital?"

His brow wrinkled. "Capital? No, village."

Disappointed, she stopped and faced the small man. "What village?"

"My village." He touched his chest proudly. "I want to show you."

"Then you aren't taking me out of the rain forest?"

"No, too dangerous. The river is angry early this season." He took her hand. "Come. I will take you to my village."

Kathleen allowed the Indian to guide her through the maze. She was totally lost by the third turn and prayed he knew his way. Staring into the pitch dark beyond the torch the Indian held, she clasped the Indian's hand tighter to keep the physical link. Beads of sweat popped out on her face, and her breathing became shallow. If he let go of her and left her, she would—

"We go up now."

The Indian's words, spoken in Spanish, were a comfort to her. A ray of light pierced the dark corridor up ahead and calmed her tautened nerves. She hurried her pace toward the beacon and felt rather than saw the first step. Taking it, she followed the Indian upward through a circle cut into the stone facade.

She emerged into a clearing on top of the mountain in the middle of a village of thatched huts. The sky was dark with storm clouds and the ground was saturated with water. But it wasn't raining at the moment, and there were many people about, enjoying the reprieve.

"Is Guerriro here?"

"No."

Puzzled, she looked about her at the other Indians, all busy with various chores. "Then why did you bring me here?" *Where is Guerriro?*

"Guerriro wanted you to learn about my people." The Indian placed the torch in a notch just inside the entrance to the cave.

"What do I call you?"

"Bonito will do." Still gripping her hand, the old man pulled her forward. "I will teach you."

Was this what Guerriro meant when he had said he would change her mind about searching for the oil? Did he think if she got to know these Indians she would leave this place? That she would forget the job she was here to do? She had always taken great pride in doing a job well. She didn't walk away from a task until it was finished. Guerriro would soon discover she wasn't easily dissuaded.

Bonito stopped in front of a hut where a young woman was grinding a plant in a large wooden bowl. A child of four or five sat next to her. "My daughter, Sashi, and her daughter, Zenna."

Kathleen knelt in front of the pair. "What are you preparing?"

Puzzled, Sashi looked at her.

"They do not know your language. My daughter is making the food we eat when the sun goes down behind the trees. You will stay and eat with us?"

The strong urge to do something—anything—prompted her to reply, "Only if I can help."

Bonito spoke to his daughter who handed her the tool she used to grind the plant. Kathleen took it and sat cross-legged on the mat on the ground while Sashi, Zenna and Bonito disappeared into the hut.

For a few moments she was alone with her work, with her thoughts, as the other Indians in the village went about their tasks with not so much as a glance in her direction. Placing more of the white tubular plant in the bowl, she ground it against the wooden sides. The physical exertion felt good.

The sky darkened. For a long time Kathleen didn't notice, so intent was she on her job. But soon she felt a drop of water on her hand. Then another. She glanced up and saw the roiling black clouds that blanketed the heavens.

"Come." Bonito said from the entrance into his hut. "The rains begin."

While Kathleen gathered up the bowl and the plants left to grind, she looked about her. Everyone was scurrying for cover. She made it inside Bonito's hut just as the sky opened up, and rain fell in gray sheets across the clearing. She stood at the entrance watching the rain, its sound almost soothing. She wasn't afraid of being caught in a flood. Perhaps because the Indians inside the hut weren't afraid. They went about their work as though nothing was wrong.

Kathleen moved to the center of the hut and sat to continue her task of grinding the plants. As she bent over the bowl, totally focused on what she was doing, Zenna came to sit next to her and hand her the plants when she needed them. Kathleen paused to look down at the small girl with the biggest black eyes and the longest lashes she had ever seen. The child was beautiful, her expression as she stared up at Kathleen full of wonder and innocence.

Something inside of Kathleen melted while she worked side by side with Zenna. The child's acceptance of her touched her heart, and Kathleen began to see the danger in getting to know these people.

She knew the moment that Guerriro entered the hut. The air became charged with his presence, and she looked up into his golden gaze. She felt as though an electrical current had spiked between them, connecting them in a way she would never understand. She saw his awareness of their bond in his eyes and she saw, too, his almost instant rejection of that link.

He looked away and spoke to Bonito in a language Kathleen didn't understand, making it even clearer she had no business here. She was an outsider in every sense of the word. She didn't want to feel that connection to this stranger any more than he wanted to feel bound to her.

When Guerriro finally approached Kathleen, Zenna jumped up and threw her arms around him. He picked her up, and she buried her face in his long black hair, giggling. The child's laugh surprised Kathleen. Until that moment the atmosphere had been somber, as if the Indians were waiting for something important to happen.

Kathleen responded to the child's laughter with a smile. "She likes you."

"Is that so strange?"

Kathleen thought about her conflicting feelings toward this man—fear and attraction—and replied, "Yes. No."

"A woman of decision."

"A woman thrust into a strange environment trying to figure out what is going on."

"You chose to be here."

"I did not."

Guerriro placed Zenna on the ground and spoke to her in a low voice that Kathleen couldn't hear. The child hurried to her grandfather. Guerriro returned his attention to Kathleen. "You're the one who came to this rain forest uninvited."

"But I didn't choose to be taken to your cavern."

"Then you wanted me to leave you to drown?"

"No, but if you hadn't scared my guide and his helpers, I wouldn't have been stranded here in the first place."

He waved his hand in the air. "It is unimportant now. You're here until it is safe for you to leave."

She glanced outside at the rain still falling. "When will that be?"

"For both our sakes, I hope soon."

"Getting tired of me already," she teased, wishing the tension between them was gone. She didn't know how long she could feel this taut pull on her nerves—this tight knot in her stomach— and not have something give. And she was definitely afraid of what that something would be.

Kneeling in front of her, he grinned, transforming his harsh features and easing the tense atmosphere. "Tired isn't the word I would use." He reached out and ran a finger down her jawline, the caress a whisper against her skin that was gone an instant after her brain registered the contact.

She didn't need to ask what he referred to. She knew what he felt because she was experiencing the same thing, because with that brief touch his emotions flooded her, as hers did him. A pure animal lust for the man that went deep to her soul tangled with an equally strong response in him. She shut her eyes for a moment as she endured the ache of wanting a man so badly it forced all common sense from her mind.

"I don't understand this," she whispered, her words laced with her confusion as well as her amazement.

"As I told you earlier, neither do I. This was never supposed to happen. We are so different. We want conflicting things." He rose, his body held rigidly, his arms straight at his sides while his hands opened and closed.

Tension instantly sparked between them, and Kathleen stood, too, to put herself on a more equal footing. "I have always been able to guard my feelings, but with you that isn't possible."

"Very disconcerting, isn't it?"

"Yes. I suggest we don't touch each other."

He nodded once. "Not a bad idea. I'm not used to a person reading my emotions."

She smiled. "I suspect, like me, you have become quite good at hiding what you feel from others."

"I have learned what I feel is unimportant."

"How so?"

He turned away, ignoring her question, which she found he was good at doing. She reached out to stop him from leaving and almost touched his arm. He glanced back, looked at her hand inches from him, and quirked a brow.

She dropped her arm back to her side. "Sorry. A momentary lapse."

This was going to be harder than she thought. She never had been a person who liked to touch others much, but with Guerriro, she wanted to, as though her body craved the connection. Over the next few days her resolve would be tested. Normally that wouldn't bother her, but ever since coming to the rain forest, she had been shifting inside, changing into a woman she didn't recognize. Boy, did she need to return to civilization where she knew the rules to live by!

"The Xango Indians have invited us to stay for the evening meal," Guerriro said.

"Is Bonito the only one who speaks Spanish?"

"Yes, he's the chief, the person who deals with outsiders. Regrettably it has become a necessity for him. He enjoys practicing with me."

"How did he know I was in the cave?"

"He knows everything. But in this case, I told him."

"Did you ask him to come get me?"

"No, that was his idea. I didn't want you around them."

She angled her head, puzzled because she had thought Guerriro had been behind Bonito coming to the cavern in hopes of convincing her to stop her search for oil. "Why?"

"Every time they are exposed to an outsider their risk of catching some disease is increased. I've tried explaining this to Bonito, but he is curious. Too much for his own good. I should have known he would be and taken precautions."

"Precautions?"

"It's unimportant now." Again he started to turn away.

This time she clasped his arm. "No, it isn't. What precautions?" His anger surged into her, and she stepped back, severing their connection, stunned by his strong reaction.

"Nothing that concerns you. The harm has been done. They have been exposed to you."

"I feel fine. There is nothing wrong with me." She couldn't help the panic that mingled in her words. She would never forgive herself if something happened to these people because of her. Then she thought of why she had come to the jungle in the first place. Would the discovery of oil really destroy these people? There was a time she would have instantly answered no. Now she wasn't so sure. "You can't protect them forever. The world is growing smaller every day. People will come. If not Dalco, some other company, one that is not concerned about the environment like Dalco."

"I know."

The sadness in his eyes took her breath away. Again she wanted to touch him, to soothe away his sadness. She didn't move but kept her distance. It was so important for her to stay separated from Guerriro and these people. She felt her determination wavering every moment she was around him. Just the reason she even questioned the search was cause enough to fear his influence was taking hold. This was not like her. The purpose for her panic changed as she sensed everything in her life doing the same.

"There's a part of me that knows I'm fighting a losing battle, that outsiders will come no matter what I do," Guerriro murmured.

"But you will fight anyway."

"I have to."

The passion in his voice drew her to him. Yes, they were very different, but there were things about this man that she found appealing—an intensity seldom encountered in the "civilized" world was one. She moved into his personal space and lowered her voice. "Why do you have to?"

His unusual eyes darkened. "I can't explain."

His scent of jungle and man filled her with a sense of harmony. "I want to understand your commitment. It's the way I feel about my job."

She didn't think it was possible for his gaze to darken even more but it did. It bore into her with that intensity she was drawn to, stealing her feeling of tranquility.

"Kathleen, it isn't the same. Now, if you don't mind, I believe the food is ready to eat."

She watched a shutter fall into place over his expression. She felt his struggle to shield himself even though she wasn't touching him. It was so strong that it reached across the space separating them. Suddenly weariness clung to her, and she needed to sit down. Taking a place between Zenna and Sashi, she made sure she was across from Guerriro. He had a way of draining her strength when she was near him—a way of making her see herself as another woman, one with feelings and passions as strong as his. A woman not afraid to show those strong emotions.

***

He was perched high in a branch, surveying the jungle below, the river overflowing its banks and coursing through the trees. The rain had stopped again, but not for long. He turned his face up to the sky and saw the dark clouds moving in. Water was the source of life, but right now he wished it would cease raining and free him from Kathleen's presence. He didn't know how much longer he could stay away from her.

It would be night soon, and he needed to return to the cave. He took one last look at his territory before starting his descent to the ground. The scent of decay and rain hung in the air. He cocked his head and listened to the quiet sounds of the jungle right before dusk. There had been a time he had not appreciated nature. Now all this was his whole life. He knew every plant, animal and human in his domain and had pledged himself to their protection. But what would protect him from one small woman who demanded he feel what he knew was forbidden to him? His fate had taken another cruel twist, he thought, as he raced through the trees toward the cave, berating a future he had no control over.

When he sauntered into the cavern, he expected to see Kathleen. Its very emptiness sent an alarm through his body. He closed his eyes and reached out with his mind, trying to sense where she was, if she was all right.

***

Kathleen couldn't believe she had ventured from the cavern, especially after what had happened to her that first night she had been in the cave. But boredom made her do things she normally wouldn't have done. Now she was glad she had explored this one passageway.

Standing on the edge of a beautiful, crystal clear pool deep in the heart of a mountain, Kathleen stared at the water, so refreshing that she longed to peel off her clothes and dive in. A crack in the ceiling of the room revealed a pale shaft of light from the outside. This small chamber with several stalactites hanging down felt intimate like her own personal bathhouse.

She wedged the torch, used to light her way, into a rock so it was propped up, illuminating the room in a soft golden glow. Sticking her big toe into the pool, she tested the temperature. It was cold to the skin, but then she felt so hot, sticky and dirty that she didn't care how cold it was. She definitely needed a bath.

Without another thought, she shed her clothes. She would ask Guerriro for something to wear so she could wash her cotton pants and dingy shirt. Now that she had found this place, she intended to use it every day.

She slipped into the water and swam about five yards to the middle of the pool. When she dove under the water to wet her hair, she felt Guerriro's presence nearby. Surfacing, she saw him standing where she had been a few moments before. His gaze fixed upon her, his expression blank.

"You shouldn't have left the cavern."

"I needed something to do." Conscious of the fact she was naked, she backpedaled in the water until she touched the other side of the pool as far from him as she could get. "Why are you gone so much?" Not that she wasn't moving, the cold began to penetrate deep into her, causing her to shiver.

"I have things I must do."

"Out putting skulls in people's tents to scare them away?" She crossed her arms over her chest to shield herself as best she could.

"If that's what it takes."

"What else do you do to further this myth about a jaguar-man? Is your—pet—part of that myth?"

"Pet? What an unusual reference for him."

"Why did you start that particular myth?"

"Why does anyone do anything?"

As usual a vague answer, she thought, and tried another approach. "I'm not used to doing nothing. I missed seeing Bonito today. Did you tell him to stay away?"

"No, Zenna is sick."

"Sick! What's wrong?" Her heart felt heavy as she struggled to breathe decently. She remembered the child's big dark eyes turned up to her, and a chill flashed up her spine.

"Nothing you did. She ate a poison plant. She is much too curious for her own good."

"Like her grandfather?"

"Yes, I'm afraid so."

"It's hard to protect people when they won't listen to you."

"Yes, I quickly discovered that. Don't wander off again. You were lucky to have found this so easily. There are a lot of passageways that lead to nothing but trouble."

"So you say."

"I don't have the time to search these passageways for you because you have decided to amuse yourself."

"What do you do with yourself all day?"

"Survive for the next."

"Why do you always avoid my questions?"

"Why do you ask them?"

"What else do I have to do?" She felt alarmingly aware of the fact that he stood by her only pile of clothes. She needed this conversation to come to an end—fast. "I had a torch. I can take care of myself. I'm a big girl, Guerriro, so run along."

"I want to make sure you get back to the main cavern all right."

"I don't need you to do that." She heard her voice crack with the thought of him in the same room while she dressed.

"Nevertheless, I will wait for you." He folded his arms across his chest as though to emphasize the fact that he was not going to budge until she came with him. "Are you going to stay in there all day?"

"Yes, if you don't turn around."

His gaze left her face for a moment and lingered at the place where the crystal clear water did an inadequate job of covering her breasts. "And if I don't?"

She prayed the distance and the dim lighting were enough to conceal her from him. "Then I will shrivel up into a prune." The heat from his look seared through her, making it difficult for her to string words together in order to form a coherent sentence.

"I'd hate to be the cause of that." He exaggerated a sigh and turned his back on her.

"I just bet you would," she whispered so low she was sure he couldn't hear her.

But he did. "Contrary to what you might think, I don't want to see you hurt in any way, Kathleen."

The sound of her name sent her pulse pounding through her body, further robbing her of any rationality. "My, what big ears you have."

"One of my many talents," he quipped.

She could imagine the teasing grin that accompanied his words and wished he would leave. She didn't want him to tease her. That made it easier to like him, to care what happened to him. "What are some of your other talents?" she couldn't help asking while swimming toward him.

"I have very good eyesight."

She paused in the middle of the pool treading water because she couldn't touch the bottom. "How good?" She glanced down at herself and realized again how vulnerable she was. This water was exceptionally clear.

"Good enough."

Her face flamed. A vision of them entwined together naked on his bed of soft leaves popped into her mind with such clarity that she stopped moving in the pool and began to sink. When her head went under and she took in a mouthful of water, she came back up, coughing and trying to catch her breath.

Before she realized what was happening, Guerriro had clasped her, holding her above the water. His touch sharpened the image in her mind of them making love, their passion blending together to form something new. Her body immediately reacted, going all warm and tingling, and she knew that if they ever made love it would be the most beautiful experience of her life.

He dragged her toward the edge where she felt the bottom of the pool. As soon as she could stand on her own, he released her and put some distance between them. She again crossed her arms over her breasts in an attempt at modesty. She suspected it was too late.

"Are you all right?"

No, I'm aching for you. Touch me again. Ease my pain. "Yes, I just swallowed some water."

"What if I hadn't been here?"

If you hadn't been here, there would have been no thoughts of us making love. "I would have been fine."

"You might have drowned."

"This pool isn't *that* big. I can make it to the side."

"You are not to come here without me."

She tensed. "When I moved out of my father's house, I stopped following orders."

"Don't make this a contest of wills between us. You will lose."

"Are you challenging me?"

"No. I'm stating a fact. This is my territory. I know it better than anyone. I know the dangers to avoid."

"I need to take a bath every day and I *must* have my privacy."

His sharp gaze drilled into her. "Then I will sit by the pool with my back to you. But I will come with you."

Kathleen heard the thread of steel in his voice and saw his unyielding look. "Fine. Do you have a change of clothing I can use while I wash these?" She gestured toward her pile on the stone ledge.

"I can find you something to put on."

"I wish I had my belongings."

"I suspect they have washed down the river to the capital by now. I've looked around the area where your camp was, and there is nothing left to indicate you were there."

If someone came looking for her, that person would think she had drowned in the flood. She was at this man's mercy to get back to civilization. What if he decided she couldn't go back? How far would he go in protecting this place? She shuddered, hugging her arms tighter to her chest.

"Cold? You'd better get out before you become ill."

"Not until you get out and turn your back."

He hoisted himself out of the pool and stood with his back to her, his feet braced apart and his arms over his chest. "I don't have all night."

Night? She was losing all track of time. In this cavern everything was mixed up and turned around.

"Kathleen!"

"I'm coming," she muttered and pulled herself up out of the

water. That was when she realized she didn't have a towel to dry off with. It wasn't like her to do something without thinking everything through to its logical conclusion. She should have realized she needed a towel and waited to take her bath.

She quickly donned her dirty clothes wet, her gaze trained on Guerriro's broad back. She remembered her fantasy about them making love and wished she could rid her mind of those desirous thoughts. She couldn't. This place had a way of making her do and think things she normally didn't. She needed to get back to civilization as quickly as possible.

Before the woman she was became lost.

Chapter Five

Before she lost all sense of time, Kathleen made it a point to keep track whether it was night or day. Using her watch as a gauge, she faithfully made a mark on the limestone wall indicating another day had passed. Her normal time of going to bed late was pushed even further into the night until she was sure that if she walked outside the cave she would be greeting the dawn when she went to sleep.

The strangest part of all this was she had no idea where Guerriro slept. She would lie down on the platform, following with her gaze his progress around the cavern, and the next thing she would realize was that hours had passed and she had slept alone. Guerriro would be gone and often in his place would be the jaguar.

Her first thought as she awakened the afternoon after discovering the pool and saw the black cat watching her from across the room was the myth was true. Guerriro had transformed into a jaguar sometime while she slept. Immediately, logic took over, and she dismissed that assumption. If nothing else, he was trying to frighten her—as he had with the Indians—into believing it might be a possibility. She wouldn't allow him to control her like that.

Rising from the bed, she stretched her cramped muscles and longingly thought of the pool and her promise to wait for Guerriro to accompany her to it. Again she felt her movements restricted, something she wasn't used to. She had always prided herself on being fiercely independent, especially after her divorce.

When she spied the pile of clothes on the stool, she knew they were for her. Lifting up the white shirt and tan pants, she was surprised to see they were for a woman about her size. A whole new set of questions entered her mind as she quickly stripped out of her dirty clothes and put on the fresh ones.

Where did he get these? Whose are they? Where is the woman whose clothes these are? Where is Guerriro?

The clean fabric felt wonderful next to her skin. She would never take for granted clean clothes or a daily shower again. Rubbing her hand down the sleeve of the shirt, she glanced up and saw Bonito in the entrance to the cavern. He moved as soundlessly as Guerriro.

"Hello. I missed you yesterday," she said, smiling because suddenly the day didn't seem so bad. She had company and a fresh set of clothes.

"The sun has broken through the clouds and welcomes us. Come and see." With his torch he gestured for her to hurry.

Kathleen clasped his offered hand and followed him through the maze until they emerged from the cave into the village. Raising her face to the sun, she relished its warmth. Her whole disposition lifted. Even hope flared within her at the sight of the sun.

Bonito swept his arm up toward the sky. "This is a good sign for the wedding feast tonight."

"Who is getting married?"

"Kiran and Maku. I hope you will come."

"I would love to." And she would whether Guerriro approved or not. She needed to reassert her independence.

When Zenna saw her, she quit playing with her pet monkey and raced to her, throwing her arms around her.

Kathleen knelt in front of the small child and smiled. "Good afternoon."

Zenna said something in her language, reaching out and touching Kathleen's hair. She glanced up to Bonito to translate.

"She missed the lady with the hair of fire. She is glad you came back."

"Tell her I missed seeing her, too."

After Bonito spoke to Zenna, he said, "She wants you to come with her."

"Where?"

"Her special place."

"In the village?"

"No, I will let her show you. It's not far."

Kathleen took Zenna's hand and allowed the child to guide her from the village along a path through the trees. When they came out of the dense undergrowth, Kathleen stood on the edge of a bluff overlooking the river and rain forest below. She could see for miles, and all of it was underwater. The appearance of the sun had given her hope that she would be able to leave soon. Now gazing out over the flooded landscape, she realized it might still be days before she could go, providing it didn't rain any more.

Kathleen placed her hand on Zenna's shoulder and continued to stare at the sea of green below her. She wished she knew the Indian language so she could share with Zenna how much the child showing her this special place meant to her. Again Kathleen felt like the outsider she was, that Guerriro was determined to make her see.

A roar like a hoarse cough pierced the quiet tranquility and Kathleen spun about. A large spotted jaguar bounded out of the jungle and stopped a few yards away, baring its teeth as its roar split the air again.

Zenna cried out and pointed toward the animal.

Kathleen's heart seemed to stop beating for a few seconds. There was no silent communication with this animal. All she sensed was danger. She quickly pushed Zenna behind her and glanced about for a way of escape.

"Don't move, Zenna. It's probably only curious about us. Guerriro told me that jaguars are normally not man eaters and are rarely aggressive toward people," Kathleen said calmly, praying that Guerriro was right. Even though she realized the child couldn't understand her, she hoped the little girl would be able to draw strength from the inflection of her voice.

Somewhere she had read not to show fear to an animal. Kathleen took a deep, fortifying breath and locked gazes with the spotted jaguar, challenging it to come forward, praying it had already eaten, because even if it was wise to run, there was nowhere to go.

The big cat moved forward, its gaze never leaving Kathleen's face. She heard the thunder of her blood pounding in her ears, drowning out all other sounds. She took a slow step back and knew she could go no farther without Zenna and her tumbling over the cliff.

Another cry rent the tension-filled air. Kathleen's heart sank as she thought the spotted cat's mate was joining it. She slid her glance toward the new jaguar sauntering out of the jungle and nearly collapsed to the ground.

Black as the night.

I won't let anything happen to you.

The silent thought pushed its way into her fear-shrouded mind and eased her terror. Kathleen watched as the two large jaguars faced each other, their cries a challenge to the other. She held Zenna behind her as she sidestepped the big cats as best she could.

Suddenly the black jaguar leaped toward the spotted one, and Kathleen felt her heart leap as well. She didn't want Guerriro's pet to be hurt. But the intruder backed away, issuing its protest as it slinked into the underbrush, its long white teeth gleaming in the sunlight.

Kathleen went to her knees, relief washing over her in waves. She didn't think she would be able to stand. She drew Zenna around and hugged the child to her while the black jaguar ambled over to them. He stopped a foot from her.

Are you all right?

"Yes, I am. Thank you."

You need to take Zenna back to the village now.

"Will the jaguar be around?"

I will make sure he isn't. This is my territory.

Kathleen had never been so comforted by words before, especially the jaguar's silent emphasis on the word "my." She couldn't explain how or why this was happening, but she didn't care anymore. If it hadn't been for Guerriro's pet, Zenna and she could have been mauled to death. The jaguar's very name in an Indian language meant "a beast that kills its prey with one bound."

She gave Zenna one last hug, then rose, her legs shaky but steady. They followed the black jaguar along the path to the village, Zenna saying something that Kathleen couldn't understand.

The jaguar paused in the middle of the trail and glanced back at her. *She thinks you are brave.*

Kathleen stopped and knelt in front of Zenna, smoothing her long black hair away from her face. "You are the brave one. You did everything I asked." She smiled at the child and again wished she knew the native language.

When they resumed their trek toward the village, Kathleen came to a decision. Even if she wasn't here long, she wanted to learn the Xango language. She would talk to Bonito about this.

The jaguar left them at the edge of the village and disappeared back into the undergrowth, blending into the dark forest. Kathleen, holding Zenna's hand, entered the circle of huts. Everyone was preparing for the wedding feast and didn't see them at first.

Then Zenna saw her mother and broke into a run. The child excitedly spoke to Sashi and pointed at Kathleen. The chief came out of his hut and listened to the little girl's explanation. They all looked over at Kathleen when Zenna was finished talking.

Kathleen slowly approached, wondering why the Indians were staring at her so strangely. "Did Zenna tell you about the jaguar?"

"Yes, Zenna says you talked to the black jaguar."

There was no way she could explain to these people that she was hearing voices in her mind, especially an animal's. She couldn't explain it to herself. "I talk to myself when I'm nervous. It helps to calm me down."

Bonito's dark eyes brightened. "I understand."

She wished she truly understood. "Do you know where Guerriro is?"

"He will come tonight."

"To the wedding feast?"

"He is our protector. He must offer his blessing to the couple. He will be here."

That proclamation produced a tightening in her stomach. When had she come to look forward to his presence? Long ago she had decided she could depend on no one but herself. She didn't like the feelings he was creating in her. The internal changes she was undergoing made her so different from the woman she was in Dallas.

***

The last rays of daylight colored the sky as Kathleen came out of the chief's hut with Sashi and Zenna to join the waiting Indians. Bonito had told Kathleen that the wedding feast wouldn't start until the sun went down. In the middle of the circle of huts, the Indians lit a huge fire to illuminate the village, casting everything in a golden red shimmer.

Kathleen sat with Sashi and the other women, pleased by her progress that afternoon in learning the Indian language. Sashi, Bonito and even Zenna had been more than eager to teach her the names of common objects. Kathleen had an ear for languages and knew she would be able to converse with them in no time. That speculation surprised her momentarily because it meant she thought she would be here longer than a few days.

A large drum was struck, signaling the beginning of the ceremony. Several men, bodies completely covered in red, black and yellow geometric designs and with bright macaw feathers adorning their loincloths, began to dance to the beat of the drums. Another man dressed as a black jaguar came out into the center, and Kathleen sat up straight, tension in every line of her body. She realized they were enacting the story of the Jaguar Man and his fight to protect them.

She instantly remembered Bonito's earlier words about Guerriro being their protector, and a tremor shook her body. She remembered her silent communication with the jaguar and began to wonder if the myth was true. Was it possible that her beliefs in science were wrong? Could a man shift his shape into an animal?

An Olmec tale described "were-jaguars," creatures with attributes of both man and jaguar. Stories about things like werewolves and vampires were just that—stories. Even though she couldn't readily explain why she felt the jaguar's thoughts, that didn't mean the animal was Guerriro. It would be more logical for her to believe she was imagining her silent communication than to believe the possibility that Guerriro could shape shift. She was angry at herself for even doubting what she had believed all her life; she was angry at Guerriro for causing these doubts. He had played on these people's superstitions to help fabricate the myth of the Jaguar Man, and he was trying to do the same thing with her.

Kathleen tried to relax and enjoy the entertainment, determined not to let anything disturb her pleasure in watching the unique ceremony. The dancers became more frenzied as the tempo of the drums built. Then the drums abruptly stopped, and Guerriro walked into the village as though they had called him with their music and dance.

No wonder the man wouldn't leave this place. He was being worshiped like a god. Kathleen remembered her doubts earlier about the myth and her anger took hold. Her gaze narrowed on him as he strode toward the chief as though he ruled everything in his sight.

Bonito thrust a pole elaborately decorated with various feathers into Guerriro's hand. Guerriro took it and raised it above his head. The Indians fell silent as the couple emerged from two separate huts, met in the middle by the fire, and walked hand in hand toward Guerriro. Words were spoken between Kiran and Maku that Kathleen wished she understood. Then Guerriro raised the pole and made an announcement.

The drums began a pulsating rhythm, joined by a flute-like instrument, and the couple moved in a slow, erotic dance. Watching Kiran and Maku enact a wedding night caused Kathleen's heart to beat as slowly as the drums. Even though the couple didn't actually make love in front of them, their provocative movements left her feeling as though they had mated.

Kathleen sensed someone staring at her and searched the crowd. She found Guerriro's gaze from across the fire, the heat of it intense. Her throat closed. His sensuous look stole any anger she had felt at the way he had manipulated these people. In its place was a deep, throbbing need.

She swallowed several times, but her mouth was parched. When the Indians began to pass around wooden cups of a dark liquid, she gladly took one and drank deeply. The potent contents slid down her throat, leaving her slightly intoxicated.

Guerriro caught her gaze again and lifted his cup in a silent toast to her. She finished her drink, her attention never straying from his compelling face. Her nipples tingled and puckered under his ardent attention. That deep, throbbing need evolved into a searing hunger.

Sashi refilled Kathleen's cup and encouraged her to take some more. Even though she already felt lightheaded, she couldn't resist consuming the second drink. Sure she would regret her decision later, she observed everyone around her partaking of the potion, and she was beginning to think of it in those terms—a love potion.

She saw Guerriro coming toward her, his long strides conveying the grace and power of the man. Again she thought of the black jaguar, the regal set to its large body, the charisma it exhibited, and she couldn't help comparing Guerriro to that majestic animal. He had chosen well the animal he used for his myth.

He stopped in front of her and extended his hand, a silent command for her acquiescence. The music continued its slow, throbbing beat as couples danced about the fire, some wandering off into the jungle or into huts.

She knew the folly of placing her hand within his, but she did anyway. His emotions surged into her—hot, scorching, full of wants—and she couldn't disguise her needs from him. Releasing her, he paused, staring down at her with such a burning look that she gasped. Then he began to dance to the sound of the flute and drums. His movements were slow, mesmerizing, his hips oscillating in a suggestive action that sent her mind reeling.

She had never thought of herself as a particularly good dancer, but the music flowed through her body, moving her limbs for her. She swayed to the beat, never touching Guerriro again, but she was so close his scent engulfed her in a warm cocoon of pure pleasure. It was as if his hands were all over her body, caressing her with whisper soft touches that left her quivering with her need for him. She felt totally invaded by the man before her, her every sense attuned to him. No one else mattered. The rest of the world faded away until to Kathleen they were the only two dancers.

When the fire and village started to spin, she blinked and tried to focus on Guerriro. But everything was hazy. When the ground tilted, she lurched forward, reaching out toward him.

Guerriro muttered something and swung her up into his arms. She closed her eyes, but the black whirled behind her eyelids, forcing them open. When she stared up at him, his face was set in grim lines, but his golden gaze conveyed the desire he couldn't bank. His emotions surrounded her. She felt wanted as a woman on a level she had never experienced before.

He strode toward the entrance to the cave system. "I should have warned you about that drink."

"It was delicious." Totally content for the first time in days, she laid her head on his chest and listened to his heart pound its own dance. "The others seem okay."

"They are used to its effects."

"What effects?"

"It can make you forget who you are."

"And you mustn't do that?"

"I can't ever forget who I am."

Kathleen suddenly wished she could forget who she was and why she was here in the rain forest. "What would happen if you did?"

"You could be hurt."

She inhaled sharply, feeling his internal battle to control his desire. "How?"

He ignored her question and stepped into the tunnel. As he moved through the dark corridor, she felt as though she were floating on a black cloud. She was still amazed at how he could see in the dark enough to make his way effortlessly through the passageway without a torch.

When they emerged into the cavern, the dim lighting from the few lit torches on the walls cast Guerriro's face in the shadows, but Kathleen could see the tension in his expression and feel it in his body. "How, Guerriro? How would you hurt me?"

His gaze, darkened by sadness, ensnared hers. "Things are not as they seem."

"Oh, that tells me a lot, as usual. Why all this mystery? I know you are responsible for the Jaguar Man myth." The surrealistic haze that enveloped her evaporated. She needed to feel only her own emotions, which were hard enough to deal with. At the moment she couldn't handle his, too. "Put me down."

He obeyed, placing her feet on the ground. She staggered forward, not prepared for the cave's floor and walls to move beneath her.

He grabbed her. "Are you going to be stubborn, or let me help you to the bed?"

She would like to have pushed him away, but she knew if she tried she would collapse at his feet. She didn't answer, but permitted him to put his arm about her shoulder and walk her toward the platform.

"Remind me never to accept another drink from anyone, you included, without knowing what's in it."

"That probably would have helped you with this drink."

"Oh, why?" She glanced up at him as he backed away from her. His image was fuzzy but steady.

"To ferment the brew they use their spit."

Bile rose into her throat. She clamped her hand over her mouth and tried to control the urge to vomit. When she thought she had, she muttered, "You could have kept that piece of information to yourself." She closed her eyes and was glad to find the dark wasn't spinning this time. She decided she was making progress and would be fine soon.

"I thought you wanted to know what was in the drink."

She heard the amusement in his voice. "Before, not after I drank it. Now it's too late."

"I suggest you rest for now."

"I'm not sleepy." She wasn't going to inform him she was just dizzy. He probably already knew that.

"So what do you want to do?"

Kiss you. "Take a bath. You've been gone, and I've been a good girl and followed your orders not to go to the pool without you. But I need a bath."

"Not in your condition."

"What condition?" She tried to stand but collapsed back down onto the platform, her hands clutching the soft leaves, their fragrance drifting to her.

"That condition." He waved his hand toward her. "I won't have you drown on me."

"Too inconvenient for you?"

"Exactly." He crossed his arms over his chest as though to emphasize his determination in the matter.

"If you won't take me when I want to go, then I am free to go when I want to." This time she stood on her wobbly legs, her chin lifted at a defiant angle.

"Don't try me. You won't win this one, Kathleen."

She stomped her foot and wished she hadn't. The room spun. "Don't challenge me, Guerriro."

He strode to her, his eyes pinpoints as they bore into her, a nerve twitching in his hardened jaw. "You can barely stand. There are parts of that pool that you can't stand up in. You will not take a bath without me in the water with you to make sure you don't drown."

"No, I can't—" She stared up at the unyielding expression and finished with, "Okay."

His expression became even harder, bleaker. "Fine. Let's go before I change my mind." He took her hand and pulled her along behind him through the passageway, this time grabbing a torch to light the way.

Thankfully the torch threw the cavern with the pool into shadows because Kathleen decided she would strip down to nothing. She only had one pair of underwear, and she intended to wash her underclothes while she was there.

She started fumbling with the buttons on her shirt and couldn't manage to release them. Guerriro swore again and pushed her hands aside, then effectively unfastened her buttons in a matter of seconds. She stepped back and began to tell him to turn around but didn't. If she was forced to endure his company and not be able to do anything about this liquid desire melting her insides, then she would force him to endure hers, without any clothing.

Slowly she removed her shirt. She hadn't meant her actions to be seductive. She just didn't want to make any fast movements because of her precarious situation. But she could tell by the flare of passion in his golden eyes that she was tempting him. When she went to the front clasp of her bra, he sucked in a harsh breath.

"Leave it," he muttered, his body strained, the muscles in his arms flexing.

She produced a bar of soap from her pants pocket. "Bonito was good enough to give this to me today. I need to wash my underclothes. I can't do that with my body in them. You can always leave if you want."

"If anything happened to you, I wouldn't be able to forgive myself."

The strain in his voice underscored what she was doing to his control. It made Kathleen suddenly feel in command, powerful. After taking off her bra, she went to the fastener on her pants and unzipped them. When she stepped out of the rest of her clothing, the air in the small cavern sizzled with the heat of Guerriro's gaze on her body.

Her desire burst through any restraints she had. If he continued to look at her like that, she would pounce on him in seconds. She had to get into the water and away from him. She quickly made her way to the pool.

Guerriro remained where he stood, rigid, fighting for mastery over his emotions, giving her the reprieve she needed to bring her own passion under control.

Kathleen sat on the edge of the pool and slipped into the water. When she turned back to look at Guerriro, she inhaled a sharp breath. Beautifully naked, he stood at the lip of the basin, sprang forward and dove into the water. She realized in that moment she no longer had control of the situation, or her emotions, and she had been a fool to think she ever had. As usual, he effortlessly shifted the balance of power to himself.

He surfaced in front of her, his expression schooled into a neutral facade. Then he smiled, his eyes telling her he knew the effect he had on her.

She ignored him and swam toward the edge where her undergarments and the soap were. She would do what she had come to do and then get out before something happened that she would regret. Why in the world had she thought she could best him? She hated the fact that he affected her on a level no man ever had.

"Do you need my help?"

"No," she answered instantly, wanting him to stay on the other side of the pool. He didn't. The soap slid from her fingers, and she quickly snatched it back up before it sank.

"Your hands are shaking. Here, let me do it."

He took her underwear from her before she could issue a protest. The sight of him touching her underclothes sent her heart hammering at a fast tempo, and she felt beads of sweat coat her upper lip even though the water was cool.

She reached for her bra and panties. "I can—" The look he graced her with was disarming, wiping any protest from her mind. She clutched at the side of the pool to keep herself upright.

He seized the soap from her nerveless fingers and began to wash her lacy bits of fabric while she watched, mesmerized by his actions. The heat pooled in her womanly core. She could imagine him removing those articles of clothing from her, and her grasp on the side of the basin tightened until it was painful.

He rinsed the undergarments in the water, then laid them on the rock surface so they could begin drying. When he looked back at Kathleen, she saw the effect his actions had on him. Desire turned his gaze to molten gold. She noticed the slight tremor in his hands as he dropped them to his sides.

"You're quite good. If you want, I have some pants and a shirt that need cleaning." She couldn't resist giving him a teasing grin.

"I think I'll leave the rest to you. You can do it tomorrow when you're recovered from the wedding feast."

Surprisingly the repercussions of the potent drink were wearing off, but the warmth his presence generated in her brought lethargy. She needed to end this before she gave him a reason to wash her body. That she knew she couldn't endure.

She held out her hand. "Soap, please."

He studied her face for a long moment, then placed the soap in her hand. Her fingers closed around the bar so quickly she almost lost her balance.

"You can get out now. I'm much better. I can handle this by myself."

"That's okay. While you bathe, I'm going to swim. Suddenly I need to exercise."

He started his laps without waiting for a reply. Transfixed, Kathleen watched his long strokes carry him across the pool quickly. He was such a graceful and powerful swimmer that she found she didn't want to take her eyes off him. She shook her head and realized she should begin washing herself.

When she was finished, Guerriro hauled himself from the pool, then offered Kathleen his hand. She was so tired she grasped him and let him pull her easily out of the water. He brought her up close to him and steadied her with his hands on her shoulders. His electric touch zipped down her length. She was very conscious of the fact that both of them were naked. Her breath became trapped in her lungs.

"I guess we drip dry," she said, needing to say something to break the sexual tension between them. She sidestepped away from him and finally managed to breathe.

"Actually I don't have much in the way of a towel. You'll dry quickly." He gave her the shirt she had been wearing. "Put this on until everything else is dry."

She could either stand around naked or she could take what he had given her. She acknowledged the wisdom in his choice and slipped the shirt on, then buttoned it up while Guerriro dressed himself.

"You're quite good at swimming." She gathered her damp underwear and her pants, socks and shoes.

He glanced up at her. "I've had a lot of practice."

"Yeah, if I must say so, there is a lot of water around here."

"It's one of my favorite pastimes."

"What are some other pastimes?" She followed him from the cavern, the torch lighting their way so she thankfully didn't have to hold his hand. She didn't think she could deal with his emotions when hers were so confused. She felt battered.

"I like to hunt."

"Hunt?"

"I do have to eat, Kathleen. Man is the only species who hunts for sport. Most animals hunt to survive. I only take what I need to survive."

"Personally, I never saw the lure in hunting animals for food or sport."

"You do what you have to."

She heard the resigned tone in his voice and was puzzled. "Why do you have to? Why can't you leave and return to civilization?"

He came out into the large cavern where he lived. "There is nothing that civilization, as you call it, can offer me now."

"Why not?"

"I'm a different person than I was when I first came to the rain forest. My place is here."

The finality in his words baffled her. "I still don't understand why you've sentenced yourself to live here."

His brow furrowed. "*I* haven't sentenced myself to live anywhere. It's obvious what I want out of life is far different from what you want."

"Did you run away from your problems? Are you hiding?"

"No, to both questions," he answered, but anger sounded in his voice, as though she had hit too close to the truth. "In fact, I go out of my way to make sure people know I'm here protecting this part of the jungle."

"Ah, we're back to the myth of the Jaguar Man."

"Yes." His gaze skidded away from hers.

"Where do you go in the daytime? I don't believe you change into a jaguar."

"I did pledge myself to these people. I look after them."

"But I've been up there during the day, and you aren't in the village."

"There are ways to look after them without being present."

"Again, the man of mystery." She wished she could probe beneath his veil of secrecy to reveal the real man. "Where do you sleep?"

"Somewhere else."

"I know that. Where?"

"I thought it best if I slept away from the cavern. There is only one bed. Do you want me to share yours?"

"What if I said yes?"

He laughed. "I guess I stepped into that one."

"We're two adults. We can sleep in the same bed without—" Suddenly her face flushed as an image of them together on the bed filled her mind. She immediately realized the folly in what she was saying.

"Without making love," he finished for her. "I learned long ago not to tempt fate. I think it's best our sleeping arrangements stay the way they are."

His expression totally shut down on her as he busied himself with stoking the fire. She realized that it was the end of their conversation.

The exhaustion she had been fighting drenched her. She walked to the platform and sat down. Glancing at her watch, she noticed it was earlier than usual for her to go to sleep, but she was tired of playing games with him. He had many secrets he was determined to keep that way. She wished she wasn't such a curious person, then she wouldn't care about what led him to live in the rain forest, why there was an aura of sadness about him. Lying down, she closed her eyes intending to rest them for just a few minutes...

With a start she shot up in bed and glanced about her. She was alone, the fire nearly dead. Looking at her watch, she noticed she had slept the night away. She put another mark on the wall next to the slashes she had already scratched into the limestone.

She stirred from the bed and stretched, a dull ache behind her eyes that she was sure was due to the drink she had had the night before. Looking toward the fire, she saw a meal laid out for her on the stool. She started for the food.

The sound of rushing feet alerted her to someone's arrival right before the cavern was flooded with the light from a torch. Bonito hurried toward her.

"Zenna is missing," the chief announced, alarm making the age lines cut deep into his face.

Chapter Six

He ran through the rain forest with speed and agility, welcoming the physical exertion as a way of wiping his mind of all thoughts except what was in front of him. Arriving at the flood-swollen river, he plunged into the refreshing coolness and swam to exhaustion. He finally dragged himself up onto the bank.

While drying himself in the sun, his thoughts—and desire—returned with a force that left him trembling. He wanted Kathleen so much it was becoming impossible to be around her. Lifting his face to better feel the warmth, he wondered how much longer she would have to stay at the cavern. He needed his life back. He didn't want these emotions he had no right to feel plaguing him.

He couldn't have her. Oh, but to feel her beneath him, writhing in passion. What he wouldn't give to experience that just once.

Catching his black reflection in the river only reconfirmed the impossible. His yellow eyes glittered in the water like pieces of gold. She would never really understand. And she certainly could never turn her back on civilization, as he had been forced to do.

When will she discover the truth?

***

"Zenna! Gone!" Kathleen thought of all the dangers lurking in the rain forest. Her heart slammed against her breast as she recalled the spotted jaguar they had seen the day before.

"I thought she might be with you. All she talked about last night was the lady with the hair of fire. She knows she is forbidden to come to these caves, but—" Bonito shrugged, the worry in his face deepening.

"Forbidden? Why?"

"The system is a maze of passageways."

"Do you think Zenna tried to come here and got lost?"

"Maybe. She's much too curious for her own good."

Zenna reminded Kathleen of herself as a child. Perhaps that was why she was so drawn to her. "What can I do?"

"We will search the cave and the forest around the village."

"Can I help you?" She could remember her own desperate flight through the passageways her first night with Guerriro. She could still recall the terror she had felt when she realized she was lost. If it hadn't been for Guerriro—

"Where is Guerriro? He would be a good one to help with the search."

Bonito looked away. "He is..."

"Where?"

He waved his hand in the direction of the entrance. "Out there."

Kathleen got the feeling Bonito wasn't telling her everything. His vagueness pushed her own curiosity to the foreground. "Where do you want me to search?"

"You can come up above and help Sashi. Some of the men will help me with the cave."

Kathleen felt relieved that she wouldn't have to search through the cave system. She would have if it had been necessary, but her fear of the dark would have been hard to handle, and her sense of direction wasn't good.

***

Sweat dripped off Kathleen's face and soaked her clothes. She cupped her hand around her mouth and shouted, not for the first time, "Zenna!" All that greeted her was the noise of the jungle.

Kathleen continued to follow Sashi along the narrow path through the dense undergrowth, wondering if Zenna had ever left the village alone before. Kathleen wished she could ask Sashi, but the language barrier was still there. All Kathleen had been able to find out since they started combing this area of the rain forest was how afraid Sashi was that Zenna had fallen into a ravine and hurt herself.

Kathleen brought her arm up and wiped it across her forehead. Taking a deep breath, she filled her lungs with the moist air that felt so heavy it seemed to press her down toward the ground.

Again she yelled Zenna's name while Sashi hacked a wider path through the foliage. Kathleen could hear the sound of water rushing and knew they were almost to the river. She remembered her own encounter with that same river when it flooded below and hoped that Zenna wasn't caught up in the swift current.

As they neared it, Kathleen thought she also heard the sound of a waterfall. The deafening noise grew louder. When they emerged from the dense rain forest, Kathleen saw why. The raging river plunged over the cliff to the jungle below, fanning out from its banks into the trees. Her heartbeat thundered in her ears like the sound of the water rushing over the edge. No one could survive going over that waterfall.

Kathleen walked behind Sashi while they made their way upstream. As they moved away from the loud noise of the falls, Kathleen began to hear other sounds, a bird calling, a monkey screeching. Then she heard a cry at the same time Sashi halted on the path.

Another cry.

"Zenna!"

No answer. Sashi began to run, Kathleen right behind her. She scanned the river flowing by her, praying the child wasn't in it. Then Kathleen saw Zenna, her head going under the water. Quickly Kathleen shed her shoes and started for the river. She estimated the waterfall was half a mile down river, but with the swift current, it wouldn't be long before Zenna would be swept over its ledge.

Suddenly from Kathleen's left, a flash of black zipped forward and plunged into the water. Swimming toward Zenna was a black jaguar, and instantly Kathleen felt Guerriro's pet's presence in her mind. Even though the animal sent a message of reassurance to her, Kathleen waded out into the river, the swift water swirling about her legs. Sashi came to stand next to her, the Indian woman's beautiful face marked with anxiety.

Worry knotted Kathleen's stomach muscles as she followed the jaguar's progress toward Zenna. He was a strong swimmer but still—She wouldn't think about what would happen if the big cat didn't rescue Zenna.

The jaguar reached Zenna. The child was thrashing about and crying. The big cat pushed a log toward the girl who clutched it. When he licked Zenna in the face, the action seemed to calm her, and she no longer fought the water. He maneuvered around until Zenna could hold onto his back, then he swam toward the shore. When they reached shallow water, Sashi scooped her daughter up into her arms, her tears mingling with the child's.

"Thank you," Kathleen said to the jaguar, knowing he understood perfectly. She wanted to throw her arms around the cat's neck and hug him, to reassure herself he really was all right.

I'm fine. I swim this river all the time.

Kathleen blinked, surprised momentarily by his reassurance.

Zenna was lucky today.

"I know. I doubt her mother will let her out of her sight for a while. It was a good thing you were here. I'm not a strong swimmer."

I know.

"How do you know?"

I saved you from drowning in the flooded river.

"I thought Guerriro did."

I found you first.

The jaguar climbed out of the river and shook himself off, water flying everywhere. Sashi and Zenna moved to the shore, but Kathleen remained in the shallow depths, still trying to digest the fact that the black jaguar, not Guerriro, had saved her.

Finally she felt the tug of the river about her calves and realized she needed to get out. She made her way to the bank. Her mind swirled with confusion.

"Do you have a name?"

I have no name.

Kathleen knelt in front of the jaguar, amazed that she was no longer afraid to be near the beast. He offered her something she couldn't quite define and wanted to explore some more. She gave into her earlier urge, touching his head and running her fingers through his wet black fur. The soft feel beneath her fingers comforted her, as though the jaguar was projecting his serene feelings into her.

"How long have you known Guerriro?"

From the beginning of my time.

"I don't understand—" Kathleen glanced up at Sashi and Zenna and realized they were staring at her strangely. They must think she was crazy which she was beginning to think might be true. If she tried to explain, no one would ever understand that she thought she could hear the jaguar speaking inside her mind.

We will talk another time. Zenna needs to get back to the village.

The black jaguar pulled back, surveyed the group, then disappeared into the dense jungle. For a few seconds longer Kathleen felt his presence in her mind, then nothing. The sudden loss of contact left her sad and wishing he could have stayed. For a few seconds more she had a hard time shaking the connection she had experienced with the animal. It reminded her of what she felt with Guerriro. That realization shocked her, forcing her to examine the possibility of the myth being true.

No!

She couldn't—wouldn't—accept that as a possibility. If it was true, then the very foundation of her beliefs would be shattered. She was a scientist who believed in certain laws she couldn't dismiss without concrete proof.

Sashi touched Kathleen's arm, rousing her from her disturbing thoughts. The Indian woman indicated that Kathleen should follow her. Kathleen placed a hand on Zenna, needing to reassure herself that the child was okay. The little girl smiled at Kathleen, and a lump formed in her throat. There were so many dangers living in the jungle. This day could have ended very differently. She hugged the child's small, wet body and thanked God that Zenna hadn't drowned.

**

"I thought I might find you here," the shaman said in his Indian dialect. "You and Zenna share a love of this place."

The black jaguar kept his yellow gaze trained on the forest below. The wind rushed up the cliff's face and stirred the warm air about him, carrying on its current the scents he had come to associate with the jungle—flowers, rotting decay, dankness. And now it seemed as though *her* fragrance chased all others away and dominated his thoughts, making him potently aware he couldn't have her.

"You did well today saving Zenna."

That is why I am here.

"Again you have put your own life in danger to save another."

I'm a strong swimmer. There was no danger to me.

The shaman laughed. "There was a time you weren't so modest. I chose well with you."

The black hair on his neck stood up as memories of five years before inundated him. *And I will pay for that time the rest of my life.* He stared up at the shaman. *Why do I feel what she is feeling?*

"I cannot answer that."

You mean there is something you don't know?

"Some connections cannot be explained."

I don't want to feel her emotions.

"She doesn't belong here."

I know. She will be leaving when it is safe for her to return to the capital.

"She should go now." The weathered face of the shaman wrinkled into a deep frown.

Not until it is safe.

"The longer she stays, the more dangerous it is for you."

I will not risk her life.

The old man shrugged. "I cannot stop the pain."

I know.

"So long as you understand she is not for you."

I do.

"That, my friend, I do not think you understand." The shaman disappeared as quickly and quietly as he had appeared.

Resigned to his fate, the black jaguar lifted his face toward the sun, remembering the first year of his imprisonment—for that was what he used to call it—when he fought the shaman's will whenever he could. Now, he realized the hopelessness of that. He was trapped here and there was no way he could change that fact. His life of late had been fulfilling until now. He had finally found a sort of peace—until now.

***

Kathleen prowled the cavern much like Guerriro often did. Where was he? She had some questions she needed to ask him. Of course, that didn't mean he would answer them, but she was determined to discover the truth.

His presence seeped into her thoughts as he slowly approached the cavern. She faced the passageway and waited for him to appear, preparing herself for a confrontation. She wasn't going to let him keep evading her questions.

He stopped inside the entrance and stared at her. She saw him suck in a deep breath, hold it for a few seconds, then release it through pursed lips. Caution stirred in his gaze while he sauntered toward the fire.

"Do you realize Zenna almost died today? I thought you protected these Indians. Where were you?" She hadn't meant to lash out at him, but her nerves were tightly strung. She didn't like not having control of the situation.

One dark brow arched. "I was searching for her like everyone else."

"Your jaguar saved her."

"I know."

"Why didn't you tell me he saved me from drowning, not you?"

"You didn't ask."

"Then you had nothing to do with me being alive?"

"Disappointed?"

"I—You led me to believe you were the one who pulled me out of the flooding river."

"I'm the one who carried you to this cave. The jaguar kept you from drowning."

Her fisted hands went to her waist. "What else are you keeping from me?"

His grin was self-mocking as he knelt by the fire and stirred the embers. "Not the hero you thought I was?"

"Hero! You are the one responsible for me being in that river in the first place." She pivoted away from him, not sure what she thought of him at the moment. Ever since she had come to the rain forest, what she thought wasn't true anymore.

"Would it make you feel any better if you knew that I would have saved you from the river if I had been there first?"

"I'm comforted to know that you wouldn't have let me drown."

"I can't be everywhere, Kathleen. I do my best. Which sometimes isn't enough."

The touch of sadness in his voice caused her to regret her earlier accusation. "I'm sorry. Today has been a stressful day."

"Zenna's special."

Kathleen sat on the stool across from Guerriro. "Yes, and when I saw her in that river, I was afraid I wouldn't be able to save her. I've never swum much."

"Why not?"

"Too busy studying while I was growing up."

"What did you do for fun?"

"I read a lot." She glanced down. "Mostly textbooks."

"So, even as a little girl you were a driven person?"

She nodded, thinking of all the times she had missed playing with friends because she was trying to make good grades.

"Why, Kathleen?"

His gentle tone, the intimacy in his gaze, urged her to answer him even though she realized she would be exposing a part of herself she kept hidden from others. "Because my father wanted me to be the best."

"And you did everything you could to please him?"

She nodded again, her throat too tight to speak.

"Was he proud?"

Again that gentle voice probed into the deepest part of her. She swallowed several times and said, "I don't know. He never said." Rising, she began to pace again, amazed that she had admitted that to him.

Guerriro's hand settled on her shoulder, halting her and swinging her around to face him. "I'm sorry. That must have been hard."

She squeezed her eyes shut and felt the comforting balm of his emotions reach deep into her and soothe the hurt. "You know, until I came here I never examined my relationship with my father. He is who he is. Now, however, I see what I've been missing, how my relationship with him has colored everything I've done."

"It's not always easy to look at our lives and see what we are missing."

She heard the wistfulness in his words and felt his melancholy when he caressed the length of her neck. Opening her eyes, she saw the longing in his gaze. It matched her emotions and melded with them. "I married a man my father thought was perfect for me. The problem was, in my heart I didn't really feel the same way. The marriage lasted two long, miserable years, with me trying to fit Tom's image of the ideal wife."

Guerriro's broad hand cupped her face. "I have a hard time picturing you being the little housewife."

She laid her hand over his. "I wasn't, and it didn't work from the beginning. I discovered during that time I am a very strong-willed woman who has definite ideas of what I want. Since then I haven't looked back."

"Except you're still trying to please your father."

She frowned. "Why do you say that?"

His smile was reflective. "You forget I can feel what you're feeling."

"How can I forget that?" She needed so many things in that moment, but mostly she needed Guerriro. "Hold me."

He started to remove his hand from her face. "I shouldn't."

She grasped his wrist, keeping their physical connection alive. "Why not?"

"Because we live in two different worlds. What good will come of it?"

"You will make me feel better. Please. Just hold me. That's all I ask," she said, weariness in her voice. She yawned. "I think the excitement of the past few days is finally catching up with me."

A myriad of conflicting emotions flitted across his face and through her. Before she could analyze them he put his arm about her and guided her to the platform. "I'll hold you until you fall asleep."

"Then where will you go?" She stretched her legs out and leaned back against him, feeling as though she had come home.

"I'll be here for a while."

"Good." She tried to stifle the next yawn but couldn't. Her eyelids drooped closed. "Tell me about your childhood."

Guerriro remained quiet for a few minutes, and Kathleen thought he was going to ignore her request. Their bond was strong, and she couldn't help thinking about the jaguar. Earlier that day, by the river, she had felt the same kind of connection. His presence had comforted her, much the same as Guerriro's was now.

What would it feel like to be a jaguar? Kathleen wondered and was surprised by the question. What would Guerriro think if she told him she had telepathically communicated with the jaguar and vice versa? Would he laugh at her? Strangely, she didn't believe he would. She snuggled back into his embrace, relishing the peace that drove her painful childhood memories to the dark recesses of her mind.

Finally Guerriro began to speak, his arms securely about her, his breath tickling the hairs on her nape. "I grew up in a small town where everyone knew everyone—"

Kathleen drifted off to sleep, listening to Guerriro's story of getting his first dog.

She raced through the rain forest until she came to the river. Leaping into the water, she swam to the other side where she stretched out on the bank and dried her black fur in the warmth of the sun, the sights and sounds about her heightened in their intensity with her keen perception.

Suddenly dark clouds rolled across the sky, blocking out the sun. The river churned, its water seething as a streak of lightning flashed and thunder roared. She changed shape. The rain now battered at her pale skin, chilling her to the bone. She needed to seek shelter. She hurried through the jungle toward the cave, tangling in the vines that clawed at her. She sensed something evil stalking her and increased her pace.

She glanced over her shoulder to see if she was being followed. When she turned back, she ran into a pole with a skull on top of it. She fell into a pit of skulls, their blank eye sockets staring at her in accusation.

Chapter Seven

Kathleen bolted upright on the bed of leaves, a scream erupting from her. Hands grasped her from behind in the dimly lit cavern, and she knew instantly that Guerriro held her. She relaxed back into his embrace, the pounding of her heart the only thing that attested to her nightmare.

"Are you all right?" He rubbed his hands up and down her arms as though he could chase away the chill that burrowed deep into the marrow of her bones.

She nodded, afraid her voice wouldn't work. Suddenly his emotions swamped her. His need for her was as great as hers for him.

She felt the woman who was Kathleen Dawson, a geologist for a major oil company, slip away. She was replaced by a woman who felt emotions and experienced life as never before. She twisted within his arms and wound hers around him. She could no longer fight her emotions, her need to be one with this man. "Make love to me, Guerriro."

He started to pull away. "I can't."

If she hadn't been touching him, she would have felt rejected, but she could feel his emotions intimately, as though they were hers. And rejection wasn't one of them.

"I ache for you. I need you," she whispered, her voice raw with feelings—his and hers—that were bombarding her from every direction. She had never in her life pleaded with a man to make love to her. But she felt as though she was incomplete and that joining with Guerriro would complete her.

He closed his eyes, his teeth gritted against the anguish of his warring emotions. Making love would only complicate their already complex situation. He was afraid he wouldn't be able to tell where she began and he ended. If he mated with her, she would be bound to him forever, a prisoner like himself. He would never do that to a woman, especially Kathleen. She spoke to a need deep in his soul, but she didn't belong in the rain forest, tied to him, no matter how much he wanted it.

"You don't know what you're asking of me," he replied in a voice rough with his own suppressed passion.

She answered by cupping his face and pulling it to her lips. Teasing the corners of his mouth with the tip of her tongue, she removed the last barrier to her heart and exposed herself totally to him, demanding he see what no other person ever had. He had opened up a hidden door inside her, completely dissolving the ice encasing her emotions. Feelings she had never thought to experience scalded her, and she no longer wanted to shield even a small part of herself from him.

A surge of his own violent need pierced his groin, seizing him with a bolt of pure, hot desire. He swore, then plunged his fingers into her long, silky hair to hold her while he took her in a deep kiss that burned him to his very soul. His tongue dipped into her mouth, sampling the sweet nectar that made him crazy. Sanity quickly faded as he stretched out atop her on the bed, covering her body with his. He grasped at his last thread of rationality, determined to remain in control and not give in to their mingling emotions that stormed through him.

"Guerriro," Kathleen whispered against his chest while she nipped at his flesh, her passion singeing his nerve endings.

"Your touch is like nothing I've ever felt. Heaven and hell all wrapped up in one."

A fierce craving meshed with his need for restraint. He couldn't explain the connection they had through the sense of touch. Even the shaman couldn't explain it. Guerriro was afraid he was looking into the face of his other half, that when she left—and she would leave—she would take a part of him with her.

But right now he had only one desire—to please her. Her satisfaction would become his, the only kind he could allow himself. He placed a tight rein on his passion, even though he was hard with his need for her, and savored the taste of her on his lips and his tongue. She writhed beneath him, her moans prodding him toward his own release. He held himself in restraint with an ironclad effort he hadn't thought possible, which hadn't been possible before her. But he found he would do anything to protect her—even from himself.

He pulled back, bracing himself on his hands above her. Their gazes connected. In that moment Kathleen realized she loved him and that he knew she did. She had no secrets from this man who could reach into the darkest corners of her heart and know the very essence of her. It humbled her and awed her.

With their gazes bound, he slipped his hand under her shirt to cup her breast. Its heavy weight felt wonderful in his palm. Right. Perfect. With his thumb he drew slow circles around her nipple, causing it to respond. Incited by her sharp gasps, he moved his attention to the other breast, tantalizing it as well, all the while still staring into her eyes.

She was fire and desperation. She was his. For a brief moment they were one.

As he toyed with her breasts, taking first one then the other into his mouth and sucking, his softly spoken name escaped her lips. When his hand skimmed lower, she was totally focused on the feelings he generated in her, on the hot interplay of their mouths, on his fingers splayed across her stomach. Sensations almost too unbearable to feel pulsed to every part of her, making her acutely conscious of all her senses. They were honed to a razor-sharp awareness of Guerriro and her surroundings, as if she could meld with him and with nature itself. His taste on her tongue, his scent of man and jungle, his steely muscles beneath her fingers, all converged to overwhelm her with a sensual overload.

He moved his hand lower to unsnap her pants. He yanked them off her in one fluid motion, then returned his attention to caressing her through her cotton underwear. She arched into his touch, meeting the pressure of his fingers as he kneaded her, stroking her sensitive core.

Somewhere along the way he removed her underwear. When he continued his exploration of her feminine core, dipping his fingers inside her, over and over, she felt as though she were swirling out of control, on fire, a blazing streak across the sky. Up and up she went until she crested and fell, hurtling back toward Earth at a dizzying speed.

She cried out his name as she climaxed. Tremor after tremor racked her body. Her pulse raced like the rampaging river during the flood, sweeping reality away.

"Oh, please, Guerriro. I need you inside me." She tore at his loincloth, wanting to feel his naked length along hers, flesh against flesh, heart against heart, soul against soul.

He gripped her hands to still them, pulling them above her head. His chest expanded and receded with each ragged breath he sucked in. In the dim light she could see the strong lines of his grimly set jaw, testifying to an inner struggle that Kathleen could feel in his every touch. He wanted her, and yet he didn't.

"What's wrong?" she asked, the fire inside her banking as she sensed the raging war taking place inside him.

He pushed himself up, hovering over her, the muscles in his arms bugling with the strain of holding himself above her. "This isn't a good idea. We have to stop." Shoving himself completely away from her, he stood next to the bed, breaking their tactile link.

"Then why did you—" She couldn't finish when she thought of what he had done to her and her wild response, her plea for him to take her. Against his loincloth she saw his arousal and knew she had affected him. She had felt it in his touch, too. Then why had he stopped?

"It was important to you, so I did what I could."

His voice, so distant, so cold, doused the fire inside her. Oddly she was fulfilled and yet unfulfilled. Sanity returned, and she felt embarrassment burn her cheeks. She had never in her life thrown herself at a man. She couldn't believe she had done so with a man who was practically a stranger.

No, that wasn't right. From the very first night he had brought her to his home, Guerriro hadn't been a stranger to her. But why was he rejecting her and what she would gladly give him?

Past rejections filled her mind, and she rolled away from him, offering her back. She still felt the heat in her cheeks, even though the rest of her body was stone cold like the cavern walls. Hugging her arms to herself, she suppressed the last remnants of her desire. In its place was a calm composure she had been striving for since Santo and the Indians had left her, since she had first stepped into Guerriro's territory and under his influence.

"Thanks to you, I'm fine now. You needn't worry about me asking you again." Even to her own ears the words sounded as distant and unapproachable as his had only moments before. She fixed her gaze onto the slashes in the limestone that marked her stay.

"Kathleen—"

The way he said her name tore at her heart. She couldn't let him into that part of her ever again. She didn't belong here. He had made that clear on more than one occasion. As it was, she was going to be hurt when she left the rain forest. She desperately tried to place a protective shield around her feelings, as she had always been able to do in the past. But this time those feelings were too exposed—raw, bleeding—like an open wound that wouldn't heal. It was too late to protect herself.

She felt him move away from her, and she sensed his confusion. Although she clenched her teeth and tried to ignore the empty feeling in the pit of her stomach, she couldn't. Contrary to the brave words she had spoken only a moment before, she wanted him even more now. And the worst part of all this was she knew on one level that he wanted her, too. His feelings of longing had vibrated through her with his own burning need. But something held him back, something she could not touch.

Guerriro stared at her stiff back, a barricade surrounding her inner self. He had approached that barrier inside her, and if he had wanted, he could have scaled it. He had come so close to mating with her. He felt connected to her in every way possible except one. If he made love to her, that would be the last connection. And she would become like him.

Anger, fierce and painful, knifed into his gut, nearly doubling him over. He had to get away from her before his resolve failed. He raced from the cavern, instinctively knowing his way through the stone maze, to the cliff overlooking the rain forest. He stood perched on the ledge and raged at the fates that had befallen him. When he touched Kathleen, they mated on a level that went beyond the physical, leaving him feeling astonished and shaken. She was his other half, and he could not have her.

He saw the rays of the sun finger their way through the dark sky. Dawn would be here soon. He already felt the sensations deep inside him that signaled the transformation. He didn't have much time.

***

Her tears fell softly onto his bed. Before coming to the rain forest, she had never cried. But even if she had wanted to, she couldn't stop the tears from flowing. She needed to release the emotions kept locked up for so long. Guerriro had opened the door, and she couldn't close it. How she wished she could. She didn't want to feel this pain piercing through her heart to her very soul.

Why is Guerriro fighting his attraction to me?

Something—someone—had a hold over him stronger than hers. Kathleen rolled onto her side and stared across the cavern. Everything about the place was different from her life in Dallas, and yet she had come to think of this cave as a haven where she could be her true self, be accepted for the woman inside that she shielded from the rest of the world.

As she scanned the room, her gaze fell upon the trunk, and she remembered her promise not to ever open it. Why? What was inside that Guerriro was so afraid to share with her?

She swung her legs over the side of the platform and rose. Walking slowly toward the trunk, she tried to fight the curiosity and need driving her forward. Her teeth bit into her lower lip. When she reached the trunk, she laid her hand on its top, wishing she could sense what was inside that he was so afraid of, so she wouldn't have to lift the lid and break her promise to him. She didn't understand what was happening between them, and she *needed* to understand.

She felt torn thinking of how important her word was to her. Yet how else could she discover the truth about Guerriro if she didn't open the trunk? Clasping her hands tightly in front of her, she pivoted away and hurried toward the fire. She couldn't do it. It was wrong.

Sitting by the almost cold fire, she determinedly turned her back on the trunk and its lure. If Guerriro ever found out that she had looked into his trunk—

She trembled to think of what he would do. No, she would have to respect his secret. The flood waters were receding; she would be leaving soon. She would have to go back to her life in Dallas and forget she had ever met Guerriro. *Impossible.* She would never be able to do that. Then she would just have to learn to handle the pain of loving a man who was out of her reach. She could do it because she had no other choice. She had gone through life never feeling loved by her father; this would be no different. What a lie! her heart whispered to her mind.

Suddenly a chill burrowed through her and straight into her soul. Feeling a stranger's gaze on her, she looked up. A small man, no more than five feet tall, stood only a few feet in front of her. His weathered brown face appeared ancient. A crown of feathers and proud bearing gave him a regal air. She felt his years of experience in the look he bestowed on her.

Staring into his dark eyes, she sensed his curiosity about her as well as his assurances he would not harm her. Slowly she rose. She didn't know how she realized this man was important to the tribe and Guerriro, but she knew it was so.

"Who are you?"

As with the jaguar, she knew without spoken words this Indian went by no name and that he had come to observe her. He looked deep into her eyes as though searching her mind. She should have been upset by that feeling, but she wasn't. His presence calmed her. Again she thought of the jaguar and sensed there was a connection between this man and the big cat.

"Do you want something to drink?" she asked, feeling compelled to break the few minutes of silence.

She turned toward the pitcher, in which Guerriro kept a refreshing liquid, and picked it up. When she faced the little man again, he was gone. Kathleen frowned, scanning the whole cavern for a sign of the Indian. How could he have disappeared so fast? Suddenly cold again, she rubbed a hand up and down her arm.

Who was he? Where did he go? Had she passed his inspection?

Somehow she felt it was very important that she had. The cold embedded itself deeper into her, and she shivered at the thought she wasn't worthy of this man's respect.

She slammed the pitcher down on the table, the liquid sloshing out. That was the last straw. She couldn't handle not knowing what in the world was going on around her. She felt as if she had stepped into a science-fiction novel where the laws of nature didn't apply. In reality, people didn't vanish into thin air and people didn't change into jaguars. There was a rational explanation somewhere for everything happening.

Her gaze riveted to the trunk. The answers were inside. She could feel it deep in her heart. She took one step then another until she stood in front of it again, her hand poised above its top. She sucked in several shallow breaths, then grasped the lid and lifted it before she lost her nerve.

Her hand shook as she propped the trunk open. The lid fell back against the cave wall, and she stepped away, fearing demons would burst from inside and swoop down upon her.

When she finally neared the trunk, she couldn't shake the feeling that she had indeed opened a Pandora's box. Her throat went dry, and her heart pounded a mad tempo against her breast. She could still turn away. No harm would be done. She chewed on her lower lip, fighting the fear, her need to understand what was going on around her. Curiosity and need won. On a deep breath, she hugged her arms to her body and peered over the edge.

The first things she saw were neatly folded clothes—men's and women's. Drawing another steadying breath, she dug into the layers to see what lay beneath. Her hand struck a metal box. Pulling it out of the trunk, she opened it. A passport and some letters bound together with a rubber band rested inside.

She refused to read the letters. There was no way she could invade Guerriro's privacy that much. But she did flip to the first page of the passport.

Andrew Stone. Suddenly, the document seemed to burn in her fingers. She nearly dropped it. *He can't be Andrew Stone! Stone and his wife died five years ago.*

She stared at the photo of a man with short dark hair and light brown eyes. The hair color matched. But the eyes didn't. And Guerriro's features were harder, as though cut from the stone that surrounded the cavern. The easy smile of the man in the photo indicated an enjoyment of life, as if he laughed often.

No, Guerriro can't be Andrew Stone, even if the photo looks similar to him. A man of Andrew Stone's stature wouldn't stay in the rain forest for five years, letting everyone believe he is dead.

Then why did he have Andrew Stone's passport? Was that why she'd been warned away from the trunk? Had he been on the expedition with the Stones? Had he been responsible for Andrew Stone's death? She wanted instantly to deny it, but everything in her world had been turned upside down, and she didn't know what to believe—or to feel—anymore.

"What have I done?" She realized the implication of having seen Guerriro's secrets.

Quickly, Kathleen put the passport in the metal container and returned the whole to its place in the trunk. She smoothed the clothes back over the box, making sure everything was as before. Then she closed the lid and stepped back, bringing her fingers up to massage her throbbing temples. There were no answers in the trunk, only more questions.

She began to pace the cavern, her nerves wound so tightly she thought they would break. She needed answers, but the only person who could give them to her was hiding from someone or something.

Finally, exhausted, Kathleen sat on the stool by the now cold fire and tried to remember what she had read about Emma and Andrew Stone and their disappearance five years before. Dr. Emma Stone had come to Costa Sierra to finish an in-depth study of an Indian tribe who had been isolated from civilization

for centuries. Was the village on top of this mountain the same
Indian tribe Emma had been studying? If so, what happened to
her? She could never picture anyone in the village harming
Emma.

Kathleen closed her eyes and concentrated on visualizing
the article she had read about their reported deaths. Had there
been any bodies found? The pounding in her skull intensified.
She couldn't quite recall the details. Then she remembered a
grainy picture in a magazine of the search party coming back
from Costa Sierra—with no bodies, only rumors. Nothing was
ever proven.

*He had told her he had come to the jungle five years
before. If Guerriro is Dr. Andrew Stone, then why is he living
in a cave like Tarzan? Where is his wife? What made him run
away from civilization?*

Did she want to know the answers to those questions?
Could she ask him? A vision of his face twisted with anger
materialized in her mind—a warning of the danger involved.
She didn't know what to do anymore and hated that feeling.
She had always been such a decisive person, but, as everything
else in her life lately, that was changing, too.

***

Even before she saw Guerriro, Kathleen knew the moment
he returned to the cavern. Her every sense became alert,
sharpened with an awareness of him that still amazed her each
time it occurred, growing stronger with each day she spent in
the cave. She glanced up at him as he strode toward the fire,
pieces of wood cradled in his arms.

All day she had debated about whether to ask about
Andrew Stone. She still didn't know what to do. She needed
answers to the questions swirling in her mind. But at what
price would those answers come?

He didn't look at her as he began preparing the food for
their dinner. She would have offered to help, as she had done
in the past, but the impregnable expression on his face stopped

her. It was as though the intimacy they had shared earlier had driven a wedge between them instead of drawing them closer. She sat on the platform and watched, trying to decide if this man really was Andrew Stone. She could not picture Dr. Andrew Stone being satisfied with the world that Guerriro lived in.

When he was finished grilling the fish, he placed her portion on a wooden plate and left it for her. His continued silence ate into Kathleen's already tattered nerves, shredding them even more.

She retrieved the plate and returned to the bed platform, sitting Indian style on the soft leaves. The aroma of the fish teased her senses, and she dug into the food, realizing that, before coming here, she hadn't eaten fish much. Now she looked forward to Guerriro roasting fish over the fire, and she acknowledged her old habits were dying and new ones evolving. She no longer knew herself.

"It won't be long before I can leave this place," she said, both to relieve the taut silence and to assure herself that she would soon return to the life she knew. Guerriro had made it clear there was nothing here for her.

He didn't respond, just picked up a piece of fish and consumed it, licking his fingers afterwards. Kathleen's gaze riveted to the movement of his tongue over his skin and thought of that same tongue tasting her, suckling on her nipples until her body was a mass of quivering sensations. Heat pooled inside her, causing her womanhood to throb.

She tore her gaze from him. "I'm sure you'll be glad to have your old life back."

When his gaze turned to her, she knew her last comment had unintentionally hit a nerve. She looked back at him. The smoldering emotions in his regard swept her breath away. Her lungs burned.

"Yes, I will," he finally muttered, then went back to eating his food with the vigor of a man avoiding all conversation.

Kathleen couldn't. "The rest of my team will probably arrive soon."

His jaw clenched, and he put his plate down on the stone floor. "They won't stay long."

"It won't be easy getting them to leave. They were quite excited about the possibility of oil here. It would take a lot to discourage them. Emma Stone's letter suggested a large oil deposit in this area."

"Letter?" He shot to his feet, his wooden plate clamoring on the stone.

Kathleen slowly rose, watching Guerriro's emotional struggle. "Yes, she wrote a friend of mine about her husband's find. Andrew Stone mailed it while he was in the capital right before he and his wife disappeared. My friend remembered the letter recently and showed me. She thought I might be interested. Do you know Emma Stone? Do you know what happened to her and her husband?" She walked toward him, intending to touch him to discern the truth in his next words.

But he evaded her, putting the cavern between them.

"What's wrong, Guerriro?" She couldn't keep the taunt from her voice as she closed the space between them, upset that Emma Stone's name would produce such a reaction in him.

He stopped his evasive maneuvers and faced her, eyes sharpened to steel pinpoints. Suddenly he pounced forward and grasped her wrist. "Why do you want to know anything about them?"

"I remember reading about their disappearance. It's presumed they are dead, lost somewhere in Costa Sierra."

As she sensed his mind seeking answers within hers, she blinked and tried to yank her hand from his clutch. His fingers strengthened their hold about her as he jerked her up close, plastering her length against his.

"Did you look in my trunk?"

She opened her mouth to deny it. His gaze struck her like a physical blow, demanding the truth. "Yes."

"How did you think you'd get away with it? I know what you're feeling, sometimes before you do."

"I wasn't trying to get away with anything. I needed answers."

"You broke your promise."

"Yes." Under the heated intensity in his gaze, hers slid away.

"I can't even trust you."

"Trust!" She finally yanked her arm from his grasp and backed away, her own anger prodded forward. "You demand I do everything you say, without any explanation. I have to trust you and accept what you do and say as the truth. You know everything about me. I know nothing about you. You take, but you don't give."

"Why should I? You just proved I can't trust you."

"And obviously I can't trust you. What happened to the Stones? Were they your victims?"

His features twisted into the ruthless expression of a stranger. "Yes. Does that satisfy your curiosity?"

"You killed them?" She took another step back, her heart beating so fast she was afraid she might faint.

"Yes. They no longer exist because of me." He began to move toward her, the air electrified with his anger.

Fear knotted her throat. "No, you couldn't be responsible. You're not a murderer. I would know."

He didn't reply but kept coming toward her. She swallowed over and over, but nothing would coat her parched throat. With his advance, she felt her stomach muscles bunch into a tight ball.

"How would you know? Since coming to the rain forest, I found I'm capable of a lot of things I thought I would never do."

The hardness of his features emphasized the threat in his words. Finally Kathleen had no place to go. Her back flattened against the stone wall, its cool surface momentarily distracting her until he closed in on her, blocking any escape. She heard the hammering of her heart in her ears. Her head spun, as fear clawed at her dry throat.

He lifted his hand toward her face.

She flinched, her eyes widening.

He froze, his gaze drilling into her.

She didn't dare breathe as he fought a battle with himself. Then suddenly he swore and pivoted away. She finally took a deep breath to ease the tight band about her chest. With several feet between them, he kept his back to her. The rigid set of his shoulders and the clenching and unclenching of his hands at his sides attested to the effort it took for him to control himself.

There was a part of her that knew she had been wrong to go through his trunk, but she realized she'd do it again if it meant discovering the truth. He couldn't be responsible for the deaths of Emma and Andrew Stone. She didn't believe him, not after all he had done to protect her, not after feeling his emotions surge through her as though they were her own. There was more to it than that, and she intended to find out what it was.

"Guerriro—"

He stiffened. "Get out of my sight before I do something I will regret."

"I didn't mean—"

He whirled about, a savagery in his expression that fit his surroundings. "Leave me alone."

The roar of his words blasted her with his warning. She took several steps to the side, then suddenly whirled and fled toward the passageway into the darkness. She didn't care where she went so long as she got away from him. His anger condemned her for her actions. She had invaded his privacy to satisfy her curiosity.

Running, hands extended in front of her, she tried to remember the route she should take to get to the village.

Somewhere along the way, she realized she was lost again in the maze of passages. This time, she didn't think Guerriro would come after her.

Chapter Eight

Damn her! Kathleen had made him dream again. She had made him want things he couldn't have. And now this. Guerriro fingered the trunk lid, feeling her touch on it as though she had seared her brand into the wood. She had betrayed his trust.

He pivoted away from his past and began to pace the confines of his present—his future. He still ached with his need for her even after knowing she had gone through his trunk and discovered things about him he didn't want her to know. And how could he face her with the truth?

She had to leave the rain forest as soon as possible before she demanded answers he didn't want to give. He never wanted to look into her eyes and see repulsion. Concentrating on his anger, he pushed away all other feelings concerning Kathleen.

**

Kathleen stopped in the passageway and slowly turned completely around. She was lost in the dark corridor, the pitch blackness closing about her. Panic gripped her. Groping along the stone wall, she stumbled, picked herself up and continued forward. Through the blur of tears she thought she saw a lighter shade of black. She hurried toward it, praying it was a way out.

Suddenly her hands no longer touched stone. The black was sprinkled with tiny lights; shapes of trees loomed below her. She took another step away from the cave, wiping at the wet tracks on her cheeks, trying to see in front of her, even though the tears continued to crowd her eyes.

An animal cry pierced the air. Flinching away from the sound, Kathleen gasped, her right foot slipping on the soft, wet ground. She reached out to grasp something—anything—but there was nothing as she lost her footing and went down.

Frantically groping about for a way to stop her fall, she realized she was sliding down the mountain toward a cliff above the rain forest. Abruptly, she clasped a plant that momentarily halted her downward plunge. Then the plant broke, and Kathleen slid further down the steep slope toward the sheer drop.

Her scream tore from her throat as she no longer felt earth beneath her.

***

Guerriro froze.

His every sense became alert. He whipped about and faced the entrance where Kathleen had disappeared minutes earlier.

At the sound of a scream—her scream—bombarding his mind, he flinched as though an imaginary fist had clubbed him. She was in danger. He could feel it as if he were the one in peril.

He raced through the dark corridor where Kathleen had gone, his heart pounding against his chest, the sound momentarily drowning out the scream reverberating in his mind over and over. Pausing every once in a while, he sniffed the air and smelled her distinctive scent lingering in the blackness. She hadn't gone to the village.

As he moved deeper into the maze, his fear grew with each step he took. He no longer felt her presence in his mind, and for once he couldn't contain his emotions. They rampaged out of control, and a total helplessness he hadn't experienced in a long time engulfed him.

When he finally emerged from the cave, the ledge was empty but her scent seemed to surround him. It taunted him with her absence as if someone had plucked her off the side of the cliff. Fearful of what he would find, he peered over the edge into the black below. His heart ceased to beat for a second, his breath trapped in his lungs.

Through the dark he saw her lying on her back, one arm flung out, her long hair fanning outward about her face. Her eyes were closed, and he couldn't tell if she was breathing.

Everything came to a standstill.

He fell to his knees. "No, not again," he cried into the silence of the night. His heart began to ache so painfully he couldn't breathe.

He scrambled down the side of the cliff, feet and hands finding the indentations for purchase. Thankfully, he didn't need to think because his mind was paralyzed with dread. Had he caused her death? His conscience could not bear another person's demise. He felt the edges of insanity creeping closer as he neared her still body, caught on a ledge, only inches away from a sheer drop of a hundred feet.

He crouched down next to her and hesitantly reached out, his hand shaking, to lay his fingers at the pulse point alongside her neck. Her life's forces faintly pulsated beneath his fingertips. Sagging with relief, he dismissed the fact he felt nothing else flow from her and into him. He could not lose her.

By running his hands over her, he determined that nothing was broken. He gathered her into his arms and held her against him while he sucked in deep, calming breaths. They did nothing to still the racing of his heart, the trembling of his body. She was alive—barely. He had to get her help.

He looked back up the side of the cliff, trying to determine what he needed to do. There was only one person who could help her now. He hated the thought of what he had to do, but he had no choice. He knew she would die if he didn't get her the aid she needed, and he would never allow that as long as he had a breath left in him.

He gently placed her back on the ground and then scrambled up the rocky facade. When he reached the cave's entrance, he ran through the blackness until he came to his cavern. There he went straight to his trunk and lifted the lid. Inside he found the rope he needed and quickly returned to the ledge where Kathleen still lay motionless.

With the rope tied at top, he would use it to help him climb up the cliff side. He slung Kathleen over his back and started his ascend. His heartbeat thundered in his ears as he labored to the top. When he had her securely on the ledge again, he scooped her up into his arms and set out at a fast pace for the shaman. If need be, he would sell his soul to save Kathleen.

And it might come to that.

***

Kathleen felt herself floating in a dark pool of water. Her mind was shrouded in a gray mist that refused to lift. The black liquid enveloped her in a sense of peace, and she resisted the voices she dimly heard through the fog.

But a cool hand on her arm flooded her with sensations and emotions that threatened to overpower her. Fear, mingled with intense need, forced her to surface.

Her eyes fluttered open, and she stared up into Guerriro's tormented face. His hand continued to stroke her arm as though to impart his strength into her and to absorb her pain into his body. When he saw her looking at him, he attempted a smile that wavered about the corners of his mouth for a few seconds then disappeared.

She moaned when she tried to move, and a shaft of pain knifed through her head. If she had had any doubts that she was alive, she didn't now. She felt achingly aware of each second of consciousness.

"Where am I?" she whispered, her words coming out in a dry cough that sent a renewed bolt of pain ringing through her skull, making the world spin. She closed her eyes while the pounding behind them increased.

"You're safe, Kathleen. I won't let anything hurt you."

"Tell that to my body." She licked her lips, tasting the salt of her skin on the tip of her tongue.

"You'll be all right soon. The shaman—"

Kathleen felt the black fog swallow her and the pain ease as she returned to the dark pool where serenity awaited.

**

A bright stream of sunlight filtered through a slit in the side of the hut and bathed Kathleen in brightness. She felt the warmth and gravitated toward it. She lifted her hand to shield her eyes from the light and brushed across the soft feel of fur.

Turning her head slowly, she eased her eyes open and stared into the jaguar's golden gaze. His sleek body was stretched out beside hers on the mat, his attention riveted to her face.

"Where did you come from?" she whispered, her voice raw from disuse.

How do you feel?

She moved her head again and realized the pain didn't shoot down her body like before. "Better. I only ache a little. How long have you been here?"

A while.

"Where's Guerriro?"

He's gone. He'll be back in a few hours.

That news disappointed Kathleen, and she knew it must have shown on her face.

He couldn't help being away. He cared for you through the night.

"How long have I been out?"

Almost a day.

Exhausted, she closed her eyes again and placed her hand on the jaguar's back, comforted by the feel of him beneath her, safe in the knowledge she wasn't alone. She buried her fingers in the luxurious fur and sighed. There were many issues to think about, but she couldn't keep the sleep at bay. It crept over her, whisking her away to that dark pool.

***

Kathleen wasn't alone in the hut. Her senses alerted her that it wasn't Guerriro or the jaguar with her. She opened her eyes to dusk's gray light and saw that tiny, old man with the feathers staring down at her. Power emanated from him, a mystical aura that should have frightened Kathleen. She wasn't afraid. She felt totally at peace.

She smiled. "We meet again."

He shook a stick over her body and said a few words in his native language. Even though she didn't understand him, she sensed no threat from him. When he was finished, he turned and disappeared through the opening in the hut, leaving her to wonder where she was and how she had gotten there.

She tried to think back to her fall over the cliff side, but she couldn't remember anything after the plant had given way and she dropped into the blackness. She couldn't even remember where she landed.

Suddenly, the skin on her arms prickled with awareness. She looked up to find Guerriro in the doorway. He stared at her, his intense eyes stripping away her guard effortlessly. Had she thought all those years that she was in control of her life?

She swallowed several times to coat her dry throat. "Thank you. I know you must have been the one to save me."

He moved with the incredible agility that still surprised her, going to a nearby table to fill a wooden cup from a drinking gourd. He knelt at her side, then lifted her up and held the cup to her lips.

Her awareness of him expanded as his arm across her back supported her weight and strength flowed into her with the contact. The mingling of their emotions was becoming familiar and no longer disconcerting. She peered up at him. The look he gave her was hot, fierce. She felt as though he reached inside of her and drew her pain from her, absorbing it. His energy mingled with hers, feeding her, bolstering her.

Is it possible for him to take my pain away? She took the cup from him, turning slightly with the action, and didn't feel the jarring pain in her head. She found herself wondering if this was another impossibility that was possible.

"How do you feel, Kathleen?"

"I won't be dancing a jig tonight, but much better thanks to you."

"I did nothing."

His gaze slid away, but she felt the shift in his feelings pouring into her. Tension, finely honed and sexually charged, sprang up between them. Something had happened that she couldn't explain that moved their relationship to another level, but Guerriro didn't want to acknowledge it.

"What am I drinking? I've learned to ask," Kathleen said, trying to ease the sudden strain between them.

He chuckled. "Water and only water. I promise."

She took a few sips, relishing its coolness as it eased the dryness in her throat. The moment she finished drinking, he pulled back, disconnecting their physical bond and putting space between them.

"I'm sorry. I made a mess of everything. I could have died," she whispered, wishing she still felt his physical connection.

"Yes, you could have, but I shouldn't have let you run off like that. I thought you had gone to the village."

"I thought so, too. I got turned around. Did I ever tell you that I'm lousy at directions? I get lost in my own apartment."

"Speaking of your home. It should be safe for you to leave as soon as you are well enough to travel. The rain seems to have stopped for the time being. Thankfully, a reprieve before the rainy season really starts."

"So you're getting tired of me already," she said lightly, but inside her stomach twisted with the thought of leaving this place. A week ago she would have given anything to be back in Dallas, in a familiar world where she knew the rules. Now she was afraid of what she would leave behind in the rain forest. She wasn't the same woman she had been.

"That's not quite how I would put it."

Her gaze caught his. "How would you put it?"

He shot to his feet. "This will not work, Kathleen."

"You and me?"

"Yes!" His arms were rigid at his sides, his hands opening and closing.

"Why not?" she asked. It startled her to realize that she never before would have dared pursue what could result in a rejection.

The question hung in the air between them. His gaze drilled into and then through her. His anguish penetrated her soul from across the space separating them, as if his emotions were so strong his body couldn't contain them any longer.

Raking his hand through his long black hair, he spun away from her and prowled the small hut. "I don't know where to begin."

"Start with who are you really."

He halted. "I'm Andrew Stone."

"But you told me you were responsible for his death as well as his wife's." She gingerly propped herself up on her elbows. "Why?"

"I am responsible. I am no longer Dr. Andrew Stone, geologist. That man died five years ago, along with his wife."

Kathleen brought her hand up to wipe the sheen of perspiration off her forehead. "I'm confused. Please start at the beginning. What happened to you five years ago?"

"I almost destroyed a whole village with my carelessness. I nearly wiped out the last of the Xango Indians."

His bleak statements touched her with his despair, and she felt his intense pain. "How? You love these people. You protect them."

"Not always. I once told you I came to the rain forest to destroy it, just like you."

She wanted to protest his accusation but she couldn't, not really. When she had made her plans to come to Costa Sierra, her only goal was to locate oil for her company. Finding it would have assured her a major promotion. She would have proven to her father she was as good as any son he could ever have and hopefully, finally, be accepted for who she was. The realization hit that, all these years, she had allowed herself to be controlled by her father's opinion of her. The hard-fought independence she had gained after her divorce was nothing but a sham.

"Emma's letter was correct? You found a large oil deposit?" Kathleen asked, disconcerted by all she had discovered about Guerriro, and about herself.

He glanced away, not meeting her eyes.

"Did you?"

"Yes. There's every indication that there's oil beneath this land."

"Thank you, Guerriro—Andrew." She tried his real name on her lips and liked its sound.

"For what?"

"For trusting me enough to confirm what I suspected."

"I went back to the capital to set up an exploration team. When I returned to the village, I brought a virus that swept through the Indians, killing many of them. My wife and I did what we could. Before we became too sick to help anymore. Emma died of complications, an infection. The shaman managed to save my life, but not before exacting a promise from me."

On trembling limbs, Kathleen started to rise, to go comfort him. He waved his hand to indicate she remain supine. Dizzy from her small effort, she settled back down on the mat, but her heart bled for him. She wanted more than anything to put her arms around him and draw his anguish into her.

"What promise, Andrew? To stay here and help the Indians?"

Again he looked away, his body so tense she could imagine him breaking into hundreds of pieces. When he returned his gaze to hers, the darkness in his eyes made them almost the brown color of his passport. "Yes."

"Don't you think you've repaid them with five years of your life?"

"I can't leave." He closed his eyes for a moment.

"Why not? You didn't do anything on purpose. I know you. You didn't want those people to die."

"But they did. I brought the illness back unintentionally, but I'm still the one responsible. I'm tied to these people in a way you can't fathom."

This time Kathleen slowly rose, ignoring the pain in her head and her weakened body. She moved into his arms. "I realize you feel obligated. I respect that, but—"

He pushed back so he could see her face. "Kathleen, I am the Jaguar Man."

"I know that. You told me that."

"No, I'm *really* the Jaguar Man. It isn't a myth. It's real—very real."

"What do you mean it's real?" she asked, pulling out of his arms.

He stood rigid as if bracing himself for a storm. "I am a jaguar by day and a man by night. That's what I mean."

"No." She shook her head, as though to emphasize her denial, and winced at the pain knifing into her skull. "That's not scientifically possible."

He laughed, a bitter sound that filled the hut with his resignation. "I would have sworn to that five years ago. I can't now. Every dawn I change into the black jaguar you have seen."

"How?" she asked in disbelief, shock holding her immobile.

"I don't know how. For saving my life, the shaman put a spell—or you could say a curse— on me to keep me here in the rain forest. He was afraid my promise wasn't good enough, and now that he has saved you, I owe him doubly."

"No," she shouted, hating to be a part of the reason he would have to stay. "None of this can be true." Feeling weak, she grasped his arm for support.

"The shaman is capable of magical things that I would never have believed if I hadn't seen it with my own eyes. This world is different from anything you've ever experienced."

"Make him take the spell back."

"You don't think I tried that at first? I finally came to accept my fate, to forget what could have been, what I left behind. And then you showed up."

His desire shot through her body like a flash flood, overwhelming her in its sweeping rush. She stepped back, shocked by the intense feelings that mirrored her own. "I don't have to leave right away."

"No, you have to leave immediately."

"Why can't we explore these feelings we have for each other? I can't deny I want you. And I feel your desire for me, so you can't deny it either."

"I wish to God I didn't feel it."

She tried not to let his words hurt, but they did. "This isn't an impossible situation. I can stay." She abruptly knew she was pleading for the most important thing in her life.

He gripped her upper arms and brought her up against his hard body. "Yes, it is impossible. I can't make love to you,

Kathleen, and that's killing me. I want to be inside of you more than you can imagine."

Again his emotions bombarded her with his passionate intensity. "Why can't you make love to me? I want you to." So much so she was doing things she would never have dreamed of doing—forgetting her job and letting her emotions rule her.

Andrew pushed her away, squeezing his hands into fists to keep from touching her. "If I make love to you, you will become like me. I could never do that to you. I could never sentence you to this life. Never!"

Stunned, Kathleen felt lightheaded with the news. Too much was happening to comprehend. She had no frame of reference for this world Andrew lived in. "How do you know that would happen?"

"The shaman warned me at the beginning about the dangers of mating. I won't challenge him to see if he's right or wrong. I can't take the risk, especially with you."

His words ripped through her heart, tightening a band around her chest and squeezing the breath from her. She swayed, everything familiar turned upside down.

Andrew was at her side, taking her into his arms, holding her close to him. "You made me want to live again. I'm so sorry about this."

She cherished the feel of his embrace, supporting her against him. She laid her head on his shoulder and drew in a deep breath to relieve the constriction about her chest. His scent invaded her nostrils, suffusing her with his essence. How could she walk away from him? She knew in that moment that she loved him with all her heart. When she left, a part of her would stay.

"We can make this work. There has to be a way. Leave the jungle with me. We'll find a way together."

He stiffened, then put her at arm's length. "No, Kathleen. This is my home now. I don't belong in that other world anymore. And I will never ask another to join me here. There's nothing you can say to change my mind."

"But—"

He placed his fingers over her mouth, stilling her protest. "Don't make this anymore difficult for me than it already is."

She wanted to say more, but the anguish in his voice and the pain in his eyes stopped her. However, she allowed her love to pour from her into him. There was no way she could stop it.

He winced and dropped his arms to his sides. An implacable expression descended as she watched him harden himself against her. "I will make sure you get back to the capital safely."

"Will you take me?"

"No, I can't leave this rain forest. As long as I am part jaguar, part man, I am bound to this land."

She felt the gulf between them widen as he brought his emotions under control. He had opened the door on her feelings and now she was supposed to close herself off and forget about him. She wanted to rage at the injustice of it all.

"Do you think you'll be ready to leave the day after tomorrow?"

"So soon?"

"Yes. If you're up to it."

She turned away and walked back to the mat to sit down cross-legged. "Fine. Whatever you think is best." She couldn't prevent the hurt from entering her voice. He wanted her gone as quickly as possible. The wisdom in that fact didn't block the heartache consuming her.

"Then I'll leave to make the arrangements." He backed away.

"When can I go back to the cave?"

"Tomorrow morning. I want you to rest some more before you make the journey."

"Will you take me there?" She was really asking if she could see him transform into a jaguar, and she knew he understood that request by the look he sent her.

"Are you sure you want that?"

"Yes. I need to understand what is going on."

He smiled sadly. "I would have been surprised if you didn't want to see me transform. You are a scientist after all, and to truly believe you need to see it with your own eyes."

"Does that bother you?"

"No. I will be back before dawn." He left her alone in the hut with her unfulfilled desire and newfound love. She placed a hand over her heart and felt its slow throb. It was shattering into a hundred pieces, and she could do nothing to stop it.

Chapter Nine

Near dawn Kathleen awakened with a start, bolting upright on the mat. The sudden movement caused her head to spin, forcing her to close her eyes until the dizziness passed.

When she opened them, Andrew was in the hut by the doorway, standing proudly, looking magnificent. Behind him the darkness of the night began to fade. Soon Andrew, the man, would be gone, and she had so much to say to him. But, as she found herself caught in the snare of his gaze, words failed her.

Once before she had experienced the feeling that time had come to a standstill, and she had that feeling again as she stared into Andrew's eyes, trapped, unable to do or say anything. Slowly she rose, never breaking visual contact with him.

A faint, iridescent glow radiated from him, and the air in the hut warmed. An energy field shimmered around Andrew and sparks of electricity shot outward, but Kathleen couldn't take her eyes off his. Nor could she move away. She felt the magnetic pull of his golden gaze drawing her toward him even as his eyes changed, slanting upward. She wanted to close the space between them, but the heat emanating from him kept her back. In one beat of her heart, he blurred and transformed into a jaguar.

Surprised by the suddenness of it, she stepped back, her hands coming up to lay over her heart. Its erratic hammering pulsated beneath her palms. She had just witnessed the impossible. Her mind struggled to comprehend what had happened.

I will take you back to the cavern now.

"I don't know what to say. I half thought—no, *hoped*—this was all a mistake."

This isn't a dream, Kathleen. It's very real.

"You've said that to me several times since I came here. I feel like I've become a part of an episode of *The Twilight Zone.*"

I didn't believe it either, until the first time I transformed. Like you, I came from a world of facts and logic. I thought the shaman had to be wrong. He wasn't.

Kathleen knelt in front of the jaguar. "What do I call you?"

What do you want to call me?

She looked deep into the black cat's mesmerizing golden eyes, and she knew they were the same as Andrew's. How had she missed that before? "Andrew."

Because it makes everything sound normal?

"As usual, you are very perceptive." She rubbed his head just behind his ear, delighting in the feel of his thick, sensuous coat beneath her fingertips.

She was drawn to him, but she resisted the urge to bury her face in his fur. Moving to his side, she ran her fingers through his pelt, long strokes over his back. Then, because she could resist no longer, she wound her arms around him and pressed her face against his sleek body, breathing in the scent of animal with a lingering aroma of Andrew, the man.

Kathleen, please, I don't think I can take much more of this.

His plea interjected itself into her mind with the hopelessness of their situation. She pulled back, sitting on her haunches, wanting to touch him, realizing the danger in doing that, realizing she was demanding he give her something he couldn't.

"Andrew, there has got to be a way for us to be together. I don't want to leave you."

I have made all the arrangements. Bonito will see that you get to the capital tomorrow.

"So soon?"

Yes. I only have so much control. Please, Kathleen, don't fight me on this.

She wanted to fight him. She wanted to shout for all to hear that she wasn't leaving the rain forest.

Please.

She heard the anguish in that one word and knew she couldn't deny him. "Okay," she murmured, feeling as though she had betrayed the new woman emerging. She didn't know if she wanted to go back to the old Kathleen. That Kathleen worked all the time, her life revolving around her job. That Kathleen had lost the ability to feel any deep emotion, feared experiencing life's passions, risking a relationship with a man who could reject her.

Follow me.

Kathleen trailed behind the jaguar as they walked along a narrow path leading to the Indian village and the cave. When she saw Bonito outside his hut, he smiled and nodded his head in greeting. She couldn't find the energy to return the gesture.

Andrew didn't stop until they were inside the cavern. *Rest. Tomorrow will be a long, hard day.*

Kathleen watched him disappear into the dark passageway, feeling her future happiness being taken away from her. A tightness in her chest made breathing difficult. She inhaled a deep breath, then exhaled slowly, but nothing eased the pain constricting her heart.

Andrew was right. She didn't belong here. She couldn't just turn her back on her life in Dallas and all that she had worked for over the past ten years. She had no right to stay and test his resolve. And she couldn't stay here and not want him to make love to her.

Her stiff muscles and bruised body gave her little choice but to rest as he had asked. Tomorrow she would go back to her old life, as he had insisted. But when she left the rain forest, she prayed her memories of this time with Andrew faded as quickly as a dream.

Stretching out on the bed, she relaxed her tired, aching body, and wondered where she would find the strength to walk away from Andrew. All the wisdom in the world didn't erase the pain of losing the one she loved. Why hadn't she been able to protect her heart against this kind of pain? She had always been able to before him.

**

Holding a torch, Kathleen guessed it to be late afternoon as she made her way through the dark corridor to the pathway leading to the Indian village. She wanted to say good-bye to everyone, especially Zenna, Sashi and Bonito.

She emerged from the cave and walked toward the chief's hut, aware of some of the Indians staring at her. Could they sense the connection between her and Andrew? She was sure they wondered about the woman who talked to the black jaguar.

"Hello," Kathleen said when she stopped where Bonito sat making arrows.

"I am glad you are well." He continued to tie small feathers to the butt of a shaft.

"I want to say good-bye to Zenna and Sashi before I leave tomorrow." A hollow emptiness washed through her when she said those words.

"They are at the cliff. Newcomers have come to the rain forest."

"Newcomers?" Alert, Kathleen straightened, trying to keep alarm from taking hold of her.

"Yes, they camp near where you camped. My daughter was curious."

Kathleen remembered Andrew's concerns about the curiosity of the Indians and what it could lead to. Then another thought struck her. What if this was Dirk Masters and the rest of the Dalco crew?

Slower than she wished, Kathleen made her way through the jungle toward the cliff, her body still sore. She recalled the last time she had come there. She and Zenna had been terrorized by the spotted jaguar. Andrew had saved them from being mauled by the animal. He had always been there to protect her, either as a human or as a jaguar. He made her feel safe even in an alien, hostile environment.

What would he do now with these new people invading his home? If this was Dirk, how would this change Andrew's plans for her to leave tomorrow? An urgency quickened her steps as branches slapped at her body, and she almost stumbled on an exposed tree root.

She found Zenna and Sashi standing at the cliff edge, looking down into the rain forest below. Zenna pointed at something while her mother spoke to her. Kathleen didn't understand what Sashi had said, but she heard the excitement in the woman's voice.

Kathleen greeted them in their language and came up to stand beside them. Her gaze followed the direction the little girl had indicated. Three boats were moored near where Santo had kept her canoes. A tall man on the biggest boat was issuing orders to a few Indians unloading the gear. She would know that man anywhere. It was her father. Her stomach muscles clenched.

Weakness pervaded her limbs, and she felt her knees give out. Placing a hand on Sashi's shoulder, Kathleen held herself upright, her gaze never leaving the man who hadn't accepted the person she was. What would he think now? She couldn't remember a time in her life when he had openly shown her affection. His emotions had always been tightly locked up, to the point she really didn't know what her father felt about anything except his work.

When Sashi said the word for outsiders, Kathleen nodded. She didn't look at the mother and daughter until her father had disappeared beneath the trees, Dirk Masters right behind him. She attempted a reassuring smile for Sashi and Zenna, but Kathleen didn't feel very reassured by her father and Dirk's presence. That meant only one thing—they had come to search for the oil without waiting for her preliminary report. They weren't worried about her because she wasn't due back for another day. They didn't even know she was stranded in the rain forest—she couldn't picture Santo volunteering that information—which meant they didn't trust her to do the job she had been sent to do.

Hurt and betrayal tangled together, twisting the knot in her stomach even tighter. Damn, she wished she didn't feel so much. She was better off shutting off her emotions. Then maybe it wouldn't be so painful. At the moment she felt as though she had experienced a lifetime of heartache in the short time she had been in Costa Sierra.

Bonito's appearance on the cliff gladdened her. She didn't know enough of their language to tell Sashi and Zenna how much she would miss them. Kathleen waved him over to them.

"Will you tell Sashi and Zenna that I'll miss them? I have enjoyed our time together, and their attempts at teaching me your language."

Bonito exchanged some words with Sashi, then said, "She said you are welcome to come back any time you want."

Zenna took Kathleen's hand and stared up at her before speaking softly. When Bonito translated his granddaughter's words, a lump formed in Kathleen's throat. Tears pooled in her eyes as she knelt down before the little girl and clasped her upper arms.

"Tell Zenna that she will always have a special place in my heart, too."

After her grandfather spoke, Zenna threw her arms around Kathleen's neck and hugged her. Kathleen blinked. A lone tear rolled down her cheek, and she wished the floodgate on her emotions wasn't wide open. She felt exposed, raw and bleeding with feelings that had been suppressed for so long. If saying good-bye to Zenna was this hard, she didn't even want to think about how difficult it would be when the time came to tell Andrew farewell.

Kathleen rose, brushing the tears away. She knew her place was down below, in her father's camp. She had to convince them there was no reason to search for oil in this part of the rain forest. But first she had to see Andrew one last time.

***

Kathleen dove into the cavern pool, came up in the middle and treaded water. Slowly, she made a full circle, taking in the stone walls that surrounded the little bit of heaven she had found in the heart of the mountain.

While swimming nude, the constraints of society fell away, and she was free for the first time to do what she wanted. The cool water on her bare skin was a delightful sensation she would miss when she returned to civilization. She couldn't see herself swimming nude in her Dallas apartment complex.

Finally she swam to the side of the pool to retrieve the soap. After thoroughly soaping herself, she ducked under to rinse. When she resurfaced, she realized without seeing him that Andrew stood in the small cavern. His presence permeated her mind, inundating her with a heated passion that stole her breath. She clasped the stone ledge and pulled herself up enough so she could peer over the side.

He was every bit a man as he stood with his feet slightly apart and his hands fisted on his hips. A scowl firmed his mouth into a hard line while his eyes bored relentlessly into her. "You aren't very good at following directions, are you?"

"A complaint some of my teachers had when I was in school."

"You're bent on doing everything I tell you not to do."

"No, I'm not. I needed a bath before I left, and I didn't know if I would see you this evening." She didn't want to add that she hadn't wanted him around while she bathed. The temptation was too much. Surely he could see the wisdom in that.

She lowered herself until all that he saw was the top half of her face, her eyes peering at him over the side of the pool. Their circumstances were difficult enough, but the heat in his gaze told her they were both in a precarious position. What they experienced between them was explosive, hot.

His gaze shifted away. "You know people from Dalco are setting up camp?"

"Yes." She needed to get out of the pool and dress before they had this conversation. "Please go back to the main cavern. I'll be along in a minute. We can talk then."

He started to say something, snapped his mouth closed, and left her alone. She took a deep, fortifying breath, then hoisted herself out of the pool and quickly dressed. With one last longing look at the water, she hurried after Andrew.

He prowled the cavern, something Kathleen realized he did when he was upset. She took in his long flowing hair, muscular body and sure steps over an uneven surface and knew she would never find anyone to replace him in her heart. They hadn't made love, but they had bonded on a spiritual level that went beyond anything physical.

Andrew stopped by the fire pit and faced her, his rigid stance conveying his troubled thoughts. "Since people from Dalco are down below, I didn't expect you to be here."

"I couldn't leave without saying good-bye."

"You should have."

"As you pointed out earlier, I don't always do what I should do."

"Do you know the men in the camp?"

She nodded. "My father is one of them."

"And the other man?"

"Dirk Masters."

"What are you going to do about them?"

"I will do my best to discourage them from searching for the oil."

Some of his tension siphoned from his body. "Will you be able to do that?"

"I don't know. My father has never listened to me in the past."

"Then I'll take care of them."

"No!" She took a step toward him, but his merciless expression froze her in place.

"I will do what is necessary, Kathleen, to protect these Indians. That is what I've pledged to do."

"Please, let me take care of them."

"I'll give you twenty-four hours. No more."

She saw a shutter fall into place over his expression, closing himself off to her. Her heart felt heavy, her throat clogged with emotions. "Andrew, I don't want us to part like this."

"There is no good way for us to part."

Even though his expression was fathomless, she heard in his voice a hint of sadness that touched her heart. "I never did like good-byes."

He began to pace again. "I haven't had to say good-bye in years. I'm not very good at it."

"Well, take it from me, it hasn't improved with time."

He stopped and faced her. "That reminds me of one thing I miss the most. A good glass of fine wine, aged to perfection."

"What else do you miss?" she asked, suddenly not wanting this conversation to come to an end. Then she would have to leave.

"The ocean. A good book."

"So all you need is to lie on a beach, reading a good book and sipping a glass of wine to be content?"

His gaze locked with hers. "That's a start. I can think of a few other things."

The look he gave her melted her insides, and she knew instantly what the other things were. If he kept this up, she would attack him even with the threat of transformation hanging over her. "I like a good book and a glass of wine, but I'm a mountain person myself," she said in an attempt to pull the conversation away from such an explosive topic. "I would like to be standing on top of the world looking down on everyone."

He closed his eyes, and when he reopened them, all passion was wiped from his expression. "Gives you a feeling of control, of power."

Startled by his comment, she tilted her head to the side. Every time she turned around she felt this man knew her better than she knew herself. "You know, you might be right. When I was growing up, I had little of that. My father was very domineering and overshadowed the whole family. I have a younger sister who has made a point of doing the opposite of everything he wants us to do. I've tried to keep peace in the family. I tried to be the son he always wanted. I failed."

"Is that why you became a geologist?"

"One of the reasons, but I do love science. At one time I wanted to be a botanist."

"Why didn't you?"

She remembered toying with the idea her first year in college and rejecting it after a visit home. "My father didn't see any future for me in botany."

"The rain forest is a botanist's dream come true."

"That's probably why I've always been drawn to the jungle."

"I have to admit that I've come to appreciate nature in a way most people can't."

"What's it like to be a jaguar?" She moved to the stool and sat, feeling the strain of the past few days draining her energy.

"A jaguar is a solitary cat. He has a large territory."

"I don't want facts. I want feelings."

"I love to climb a tall tree and survey the forest. I love to swim in the river, to feel the water against my fur."

"Until you rescued Zenna, I didn't realize jaguars were such good swimmers."

"It comes in handy in the jungle, especially during the rainy season." He laughed and eased down on the other stool across from her. "I can't believe I'm talking to another person about being a jaguar. I've kept that secret for so long. The Indians suspect, but they really don't know for sure. It isn't something we discuss. I think they are afraid to."

"They are in awe of you."

"They are in awe of the Jaguar Man."

She compared Andrew to a jaguar and saw many similarities. Both were protective, territorial and strong. But most of all they were loners. He had learned to need no one because that luxury was denied him.

Andrew rested his elbows on his thighs and clasped his hands together, leaning slightly forward. "Over the years of our relationship, they have come to trust me. Even after I was responsible for so many of their deaths."

"You didn't do anything on purpose. How long are you going to punish yourself for something you couldn't control?"

"I can never forget it, Kathleen."

"How about forgiving yourself? From what you say, the tribe has. Don't you think it's time you forgave yourself?"

"When I've paid my debt."

"Who decides that?"

Andrew shrugged. "I will know in my heart."

"In the meantime, you've given them your life."

"That's all I have left to give."

She felt her heart ripping in two. One part would always remain with Andrew. "Are you sure about me—"

"Don't, Kathleen. We have been over this before. My mind is made up. There isn't anything you can do about it." He shot to his feet, tension in every line of his body.

"How do you know what I was going to say?" She rose but kept her distance.

"You forget that we are connected."

"No, that's the problem. I'll never be able to forget that," she murmured, her throat closing around the words.

"Neither will I," he whispered, his voice rough.

She reached out to touch him. He flinched away.

"I can't handle that, Kathleen." His chest expanded with a deep breath. "Now, if you're ready, I'll take you to your father."

No! She didn't want to leave just yet. She sank back down onto the stool, her legs weak, her mind numb with what must be done. "Let me rest a while longer."

"Kathleen."

"I promise I will go later this evening. I agree. We shouldn't prolong this much longer. It will make everything so much harder."

"Then perhaps I should leave and return in a while."

"No, please don't, Andrew." She hated the plea in her voice, but she couldn't ignore the deep ache in her heart that demanded every second possible be spent with him. "Stay and tell me about your life as Andrew Stone. I know a few details from when you and Emma disappeared. The newspapers carried the story for a couple of days, until some other disaster occurred in another part of the world."

He looked at her warily.

She lifted her chin and dared him to deny her last request.

Some of his tension eased, and he sat again on the stool across from her. "I led a rather boring life. Like you, I loved science. I found everything fascinating. It was difficult to pick what field to go into, but I was newly married and needed to make a decent living. I chose geology. But I have to admit Emma's work was interesting to me, too. That was why I came with her to Costa Sierra."

"She was garnishing quite a reputation in her field. My friend at the University of Texas whom she wrote felt she had a great future in anthropology, especially her work with the Indian tribes of this region."

"I didn't come to the rain forest looking for oil, but I stumbled over a large oil seep. Being the geologist I was, I couldn't ignore the signs and walk away. I couldn't leave well enough alone."

She frowned. "Is it possible to see the oil seep?"

"No. I took great pains to hide any obvious evidence of oil."

"Good."

He cocked his head to the side. "Does that mean you aren't going to push for Dalco to explore here?"

"I told you I would get them to leave. That is if I can convince the others Emma's letter was a fool's errand."

"What happened to the woman who was all work when she came here? Nothing was going to get in your way, not even me."

"I think she drowned in the river the first day." Kathleen paused. "I'm a different person now. And that fact won't change."

His eyes glittered at her words, but he remained silent.

"Andrew, you do realize you can't keep people away for long."

"Yes."

"There are ways to drill for oil that are environmentally friendly."

"Yes, I realize there are, but not all companies do."

"More and more are being forced to."

"That still doesn't protect these Indians."

"If they are slowly introduced to the outside world, they might develop some immunities to our common diseases. And there are medicines to help them with that."

"Possibly. It's a shame that hundreds of years can be wiped away in a few."

"That's called progress."

"If progress comes to this rain forest, then I will be here to help ease the transition."

She took a moment to study him, to memorize everything she could about him. It would have to last her a lifetime. What appealed to her the most, she decided, was his intense caring, his protectiveness. She had never had that in her life—someone she could depend on no matter what.

"I love you, Andrew." The words came out in a whisper that no one would have heard except someone with exceptional hearing.

"Kathleen, I—" He swallowed hard. "I wish my life was different. It isn't."

"I know. I just wanted you to know how I feel. I wanted you to hear it from me. I don't usually express my feelings. Please kiss me good-bye."

His gaze widened. "I can't."

"Please."

He looked long and hard at her, indecision warring in his eyes. "I will when I take you back to your camp. Are you ready now?"

"My, a gal could think you want to get rid of her."

He surged to his feet, waiting.

Slowly she rose and followed him from the cavern. At the entrance she paused for a moment and glanced back at the place that had been a home to her for a while. She realized the cavern meant more to her than her Dallas apartment. She turned away and continued after Andrew, who held a torch to light the way.

When they reached the outskirts of the camp, Andrew stopped, the dense foliage camouflaging them from the people's

view. She watched her father talking with Dirk. Her father
looked older than she remembered, and yet she had seen him
right before she left to come here. She had often seen him
frown, but there was something else in his expression that
concerned her.

"Kathleen, this is where we need to say good-bye."

Andrew came up behind her and laid his hands on her
shoulders. The instant connection poured into her, and she was
drowning in their intermingling emotions. She swayed back
against him, forgetting for the moment that there were people
not ten yards away.

He turned her to face him and lifted her chin. She didn't
have to see his expression to know what was in it. She felt it
deep inside her, the love, the desire. Her heart broke.

Holding her face, he slanted his mouth and took hers in a
kiss that rocked her to her core. He pulled her against him,
their minds merging as one, their bodies touching every place
they could. His fingers delved into the thick strands of her hair
while she clutched him to keep herself from collapsing.

She wanted so much more, and she projected that need to
him. He swore softly and rained kisses along her cheek to her
ear, where he nibbled on its lobe.

"Oh, Kathleen, I wish things were different," he whispered
while devouring her with drugging kisses.

"I don't want to let you go." She tossed her head back so he
could taste her neck.

"We have no choice, darling."

He licked the hollow pulse point in her throat, and
Kathleen moaned, her insides dissolving with her unfulfilled
needs.

"Did you hear something?"

Dirk's question brought Andrew's head up. Kathleen felt
abandoned in that moment when he determinedly placed her
away from him then lowered his hands to his sides.

"Good-bye," Andrew whispered and faded into the undergrowth.

"Don't ever forget I love you," Kathleen mouthed the words, wishing she could see into the dark.

Moments later she knew Andrew wasn't going to come up and whisk her off to the cave. He was gone for good. She turned toward the camp as her father stood and surveyed the jungle around him.

"I think you're imagining things," her father said, but his frown was deep. "Don't tell me you believe that myth about the Jaguar Man."

"Of course not," Dirk scoffed. "No, I thought I heard someone moaning."

"Just your imagination."

Kathleen almost laughed out loud. She would never tell them the truth about Andrew. But if they only knew.

"Come on, let's look at that map. We need to plan our strategy." Her father sat again in his canvas chair.

Kathleen knew it was time for her to see him, but a part of her held back. When she entered the camp, she would be going back to her old life. How was the new Kathleen going to survive, living without Andrew?

Chapter Ten

Inhaling deeply, Kathleen strolled into the middle of the campsite as though she belonged and had only been gone for a few minutes—not days. When her father glanced up at her, a startled expression on his face, she smiled. Inside, she quaked with the struggle to control frazzled nerves, anger, and deeply felt needs.

"Good evening, Dad, Dirk." Amazingly, her voice sounded strong—especially since her mouth and throat felt parched and her body dripped sweat.

"Kathleen?" Dirk sounded as though he couldn't believe she stood in front of him.

"That's what my passport says," she quipped, not sure what else to say at both men's stunned looks.

For a long moment her father said nothing, then he bolted to his feet, the map in his lap floating to the ground. "Where the hell have you been?"

She winced but held her ground, a few feet from him. "I've been here doing my job. Where else would I be?" she replied in the calmest voice she could muster, still fighting for that control that used to come to her so effortlessly, even when dealing with her father.

"No, you've been lost." Her father snatched up the map.

"Where did you get an idea like that?"

"From your guide!" her father yelled, anger replacing the tired lines about his eyes and mouth.

"Santo?"

"Yes! Remember he did work for Dalco here in Costa Sierra."

She was surprised that her father was shouting. He always had such a firm control on his temper. "Do you want me to leave and go back where I was?" She almost hoped he would answer "yes."

"Just where the hell was that?"

Her own anger, which she'd kept reined in for years when dealing with him, swamped her. She clenched her teeth and hands while she tried to think of the best answer. "I was with the local Indians. They assisted me when Santo and his helpers abandoned me. Are you disappointed I survived? Is that what this is all about?" She would never have challenged her father before, but she wasn't the old Kathleen.

"Of course not. Why would you say something like that?"

"Because you're yelling at me." Even though her instinct to soothe, to compromise, began to surface, she pushed it back down. She'd done nothing wrong and would not be made to feel she had.

He glared at her for a moment, then sat down in his canvas chair, refolding the map he held haphazardly. "Well, Dirk, we have one less thing to look for. Now we can get down to business and concentrate on searching for that oil. We have money to make."

His quick dismissal pierced her, and she felt the rejection, completely and devastatingly. But this time she wasn't going to slink away and lick her wounds. "Why are you angry with me?"

He stabbed her a narrowed gaze, his hard expression telling her she should already know the answer.

"I think I'll leave you two to discuss this matter," Dirk interjected into the stress-laden air. "I have some things to discuss with our Indian helpers."

Kathleen vaguely sensed Dirk walking away, but her full attention was riveted on her father. He seemed to be wrestling with something. A gamut of emotions flitted across his expression, surprising her. He usually showed nothing but displeasure. Not even anger. Was there something magical about this rain forest that made people do—feel—things they normally didn't?

"I want to know what's going on here, Dad. You weren't supposed to come to Costa Sierra."

He looked away, his mouth thinning. "I was worried about you."

"You were?" Her eyes widened.

"Is that such a surprise?"

"Yes."

A defensive edge entered his voice. "You're my daughter, and you were missing."

"No, I wasn't. I was right where I was supposed to be."

"Santo told me about the flood."

"He did?" Kathleen couldn't imagine the man admitting to leaving her here by herself.

"When Dirk arrived, he found Santo, drunk, and demanded some answers from him. Once Dirk got them, he contacted me, said you were missing. That the river had flooded."

"Where's Santo now?"

Again her father's gaze slipped away. "He's in the hospital."

"Why?"

He grimaced. "I beat him up."

"You did?"

"When I heard what he had done, I sort of lost it. He left you stranded in the middle of a damn jungle. He *worked* for us."

Kathleen had to sit down. Her legs felt weak, her whole body shaking. Her father never lost control. She asked the first thing she could think of, which had nothing to do with what she really wanted to know. "Dirk wasn't due for a few more days. Why did he come early?"

"I asked him to."

"Because you didn't trust me?"

"Not quite. I did regret allowing you to come here. You're unfamiliar with this kind of terrain. I took Dirk off his other assignment so he could join up with you earlier than planned. He should have been here with you from the beginning. I was right. You got into some trouble."

This was familiar territory between them. She could understand him not thinking she could do the job. That thought hurt but didn't surprise her. This time, however, she did nothing to conceal her feelings about his words.

"Not because I wasn't capable," she fired back, hurt and anger evident in her voice. "What happened was out of my control. It could have happened to anyone, even you. Dirk being here wouldn't have stopped the flood. Does he have some kind of skill I don't know about?"

Her father's gaze bored into her, but it didn't make her shrink away, not after experiencing Andrew's similar attempts to intimidate. She met his look with her own unwavering one.

"Okay, I admit what happened to you could happen to anyone."

"Thank you. That's a start."

"A start?"

"Yes. For years I've tried to do everything the way you wanted. And you never bothered to thank me. To tell me you cared." Now that her emotions were opened up, she let them pour out of her.

Her father blinked, his eyes round.

"I can't remember when you praised me for anything, but I can remember every time you criticized me. I'm sorry I wasn't the son you wanted, but that's life. Adjust, make the best of the situation and move on."

He rose slowly, almost as though his age were finally catching up with him. "Is that what you thought? I won't deny there was a time I wanted a son to carry on my name, but long ago I came to terms with the fact I had two daughters."

Kathleen crossed her arms over her chest, not three feet away from her father, but it might as well have been a canyon. "That's news to me. From where I stood, it certainly looked like you were disappointed with everything I did. I graduated from college in the top five percent of my class, but you wanted to know why I wasn't valedictorian. I got my doctorate in two years, but you thought I should have finished faster. Should I go on?"

"I wanted you to do your best."

"Don't you get it? I was!" Kathleen pivoted away, looking for a place to escape to. "Why did you even bother coming down here?"

"I don't understand what is happening here. You've never acted this way before, Kathleen."

She hugged her arms tighter to her body, fighting the need to cry. She would not cry in front of her father and let him see how much his years of rejection affected her. She shoved down the emotions threatening to choke her. "I've learned a few things lately."

"What are you talking about?"

She shook her head. "Never mind. Where can I sleep? I'm suddenly very tired." Her head throbbed, and she was exhausted.

"I guess Dirk and I can share a tent. You can have mine."

She heard her father move toward her, and she stiffened.

"Listen, Kathleen, we'll talk tomorrow morning before we start our search."

"Yes, we'll talk then," she murmured, wondering what good it would do. "Where's your tent?"

"There."

She glanced over her shoulder to see where her father pointed, then headed toward the tent. All she wanted to do was sleep. Emotions demanded a lot of energy, she thought, while she sank down onto his cot and pulled the netting over her. As she felt sleep descend, her mind swirled with images of Andrew and the black jaguar, two distinct figures that slowly melted into one.

***

"It's a waste of our time to stay any longer," Kathleen said the next morning. "I was wrong." She sipped her coffee, sitting with her father and Dirk, the map spread on the ground in front of them.

"But the letter stated there were large oil seeps in this area." Her father scowled at her. "Andrew Stone was very good at finding oil."

"I haven't found any, and I've searched everywhere. There's no indication of oil within the seismic lines. There's no indication of faulting and there is no source rock. This was a wild goose chase and a waste of good money."

"You did all this by yourself?"

Her father's question sparked her anger. "Yes, I do have my doctorate in geology. I do know how to look for the existence of oil." She drew herself up straight, her chin lifted at a proud angle. All she had said was true, lacking a few important details. Such as, she hadn't been much farther than Andrew's cave and the Indian village.

"Where's your equipment?"

"Lost in the flood."

"Then how did you run all those tests?"

"I was able to use the equipment to test before the flood," she answered, hoping the confrontation with Santo hadn't been so detailed that he knew she'd been on her own after the first day.

"I would still like to have a look around the area since we came all this way."

"I thought you came looking for me."

"Well, yes, but the oil, too."

"Of course." She almost asked if he had come primarily for the oil, with her an inconvenient afterthought, but she really didn't want him to confirm what she already knew. She would always come in second in his life behind his work.

He stood and looked down at her. "Aren't you coming with us?" Her father's glance took in the silent Dirk, who had kept his attention focused on the map during the conversation.

"No, the last few weeks have taken their toll. I'm going to rest. I've checked the area and didn't find anything. I don't need to check it again."

"Suit yourself." Her father walked off with Dirk.

Kathleen waited until everyone left camp, then jumped up and headed into the dense undergrowth in the opposite direction. She prayed she could remember how to get to Andrew's cave because she had to see him. She couldn't talk her father out of searching for the oil. She should have known that, but she'd hoped for once he'd listen to her.

Walls of green closed in around her as she moved deeper into the rain forest, reinforcing her feeling of total isolation. She managed to keep her gaze on the cliff ahead, a monkey high in a tall tree shrieked. She gasped and turned toward the sound, still not used to the howler monkey's sudden intrusion into the subdued atmosphere of the rain forest floor.

Once her pulse slowed sufficiently, she continued to the base of the cliff. The rock surface looked unfamiliar. And even if she could find the entrance Andrew used, she would get lost in the passageways. She needed to get to the Indian village and enter the cave from there. Again she inspected the cliff for the path the Indians took. Small footholds in the rock indicated a staircase they utilized, but Kathleen wasn't sure she could make it to the top in her present condition. But she had no other choice at the moment.

Time was critical. She needed to be back in camp before her father and Dirk returned. Placing a foot in the first indentation, she hoisted herself upward. Again and again. Sweat drenched her face and ran down her body. Periodically, she dried her hands on her clothes to keep her grip firm.

She was about a fourth of the way to the top when she felt a presence touch her mind. She halted in mid-reach.

Kathleen, what are you doing?

She glanced down and almost lost her grip. Steadying herself, she blew out a relieved breath and looked toward the forest floor. Andrew, in jaguar form, sat on his haunches, his head angled upward, those yellow eyes penetrating.

Please come down. That path isn't used anymore.

"Now he tells me," she muttered and started her slow descent.

You never asked.

"I keep forgetting what big ears you have." She swore she thought she heard him chuckle. "Glad you think this is funny. I think I'm stuck."

No, you're not. There's a foothold right below your right foot. Ease down.

"Easy for you to say. I think I've suddenly developed a fear of heights."

Not you, Kathleen. You're capable of anything.

Delight at his confidence in her ability nudged all other feelings aside. Kathleen followed Andrew's instructions all the way down, and when she finally reached the ground, she collapsed onto a rock, bending over and drawing in deep breaths. "I can't believe I tried that."

Why did you?

"I needed to see you, and I couldn't think of any other way than to come to the cave."

What's wrong?

"My father and Dirk decided to look for the oil."

I know.

"Aren't you worried?"

They're going in the wrong direction. They won't find anything today.

"But I can't stop them from searching the whole area. I tried."

Yes, I heard.

"You were near and let me come all this way?"

Actually, I followed them for a while. When I came back to the campsite, you were gone. I came looking for you, thankfully. I didn't think you would try something like this. Obviously I was wrong.

"I'm going to ignore that remark. What are we going to do?"

We aren't going to do a thing.

"Okay, let me rephrase that question. What are *you* going to do?" She wanted to touch him, to feel his soft fur beneath her hands and connect with him again on the only level she could.

Conjure up another flood?

"You didn't?"

Another chuckle sounded in her mind. *No. I may have many talents, but not that one. Of course, I wouldn't put it past the shaman to have the ability.*

"He can do that?"

I don't know for sure. He does have powers I can't fathom.

"I don't want my father hurt. Isn't there something I could do?"

Maybe.

"What?" Kathleen knelt in front of Andrew and finally touched the fur behind his neck.

He rubbed against her hand, his emotions sweeping through her. Ecstasy. She laid her head on his back and stroked him, relishing the bond for the few moments he would allow. When his desire became so strong that it overwhelmed all other emotions, he moved away.

Come, let me think about this while I escort you back to your camp.

Bereaved, Kathleen took a moment to gather her poise. Her hands shook from the brief contact with Andrew. Her body felt empty when his emotions rushed out of her. Slowly she pushed herself to her feet and followed him through the rain forest.

When Andrew came to the outskirts of the camp, he stopped. *Are you sure you want to help me?*

"As long as it won't hurt my father."

Then I have a way. I'll bring you a potion tonight that will make you unconscious. It won't harm you, but they will think something is wrong with you and hopefully decide to return to the capital to get you some medical help. The potion lasts between one and two days.

"What if they don't leave?"

Your father cared enough to come all the way to Costa Sierra to look for you. He'll leave.

Kathleen wasn't so sure, but she was willing to try it because she didn't want anything to happen to either her father or Andrew. If they went head to head, someone would get hurt. "Okay, I'll do it. You'll bring it here tonight after dark?"

Yes.

"How will I know you're here?"

Kathleen, you'll know. You haven't forgotten our connection so soon, have you?

"Yes, you're right." She always sensed he was near even before she saw him.

I'll have the potion. You should take it right before everyone gets up tomorrow morning.

"Kathleen, don't move. I've got the jaguar in my sights."

Her father's voice shattered Andrew's presence in her mind. She whirled about to find her father on the other side of the camp, his rifle aimed at Andrew's head. Her heart seemed to stop for a few seconds, then began to hammer, its tempo out of control.

"Move slightly to the side, so I can get a good shot."

"No!" Kathleen threw herself completely in front of Andrew. "I know this jaguar."

"What do you mean? He's a wild animal."

"He's my friend. He saved my life in the flood."

Her father relaxed his grip on his rifle but didn't bring it down. "Friend? An animal? How in the world did he save your life?"

"He pulled me from the water. Please put the rifle down, Dad." She could feel Andrew's tension as though it was hers.

Slowly, almost reluctantly, her father dropped the gun to his side. "This is hard to believe."

Kathleen knelt beside Andrew and put her arms around his neck, burying her face in his fur for a few seconds and taking a deep breath of his animal scent. She had almost lost him. "See, he's harmless." The surge of his emotions into her made her voice weak, her body quiver.

"What's been going on since you came here?" Her father kept his distance, his gaze alert, wary, his finger still poised on the trigger.

"When Santo abandoned me, I got caught in a flood. This jaguar rescued me. As I told you, the Indians of the area took me in."

"And that's all? You seem different."

She could never explain to him how much she'd changed. He'd never understand. "I'm the same person I was when I came to the rain forest. Dr. Kathleen Dawson, geologist for Dalco, your daughter." She felt Andrew move beneath her touch and heard his good-bye in her mind. She fought the urge to grasp him and keep him at her side. Instead, she watched him stare up at her father for a moment, then saunter into the dense foliage as though he owned the rain forest.

Her father visibly relaxed after Andrew left, his finger easing off the trigger. "I hope he isn't going to pay us another visit."

"Where's everyone else?"

"They're coming. We're going to try the other direction." She shrugged. "Suit yourself. It's a waste of time, but then it's your time."

"Why don't you come with us?"

"I'd rather stay here." She walked to a canvas chair and sat as though to emphasize that she wasn't going anywhere.

"I don't like leaving you behind alone."

"I'm perfectly safe."

He waved his hand in the direction Andrew had disappeared. "What if he's not the only jaguar around? What if he decides to turn on you?"

"Jaguars are rarely seen, Dad. Besides, this is his territory and he would never turn on me." She said it with such confidence that her father's eyebrows rose.

"You seem to know quite a bit about this animal."

"The Indians told me about him. He did save my life."

He made a sound deep in his throat, as if he couldn't quite believe all she had said. She looked away, not meeting his gaze, uncertain whether she could keep the truth from showing.

"Then at least get the other rifle from my tent and carry it. You remember how to shoot, don't you?"

"Yes," she replied as the others came into camp.

***

She leaped onto the lower branch and climbed as high as she could go. Perched in a crook of the tree, she surveyed the rain forest below. She felt the sunlight that filtered through the broad leaves kiss her fur, the hot, humid air making her lethargic. She would hunt at night in the coolness when she would blend in with the dark.

A flash of black caught her eye as her mate scaled the tree trunk and came to rest alongside her, his powerful body nestled against hers. She purred in contentment.

Suddenly Kathleen felt a hand clamp over her mouth, heard a rough whisper in her ear, beckoning her to awaken. Her eyes flew open.

Andrew! He had come finally. She couldn't see him in the dark, but could feel his presence like a warm, comforting blanket in the dead of winter.

He lifted his hand from her mouth and would have moved away except that Kathleen gripped his arm to hold him close. She didn't want the connection broken just yet.

"I'd given up hope you would be here tonight. I should have realized you would come after everyone was asleep."

"Safer. I thought it would be hard for you to explain taking a walk in the jungle after refusing to all day."

She smiled. "Yeah, I'd better not give my father any more cause for concern. Frankly, after you left today, he kept giving me strange looks. Like I had gone crazy befriending a jaguar."

"I brought you the potion. Make sure you take it right before everyone awakens. Once you regain consciousness you will recover rapidly with no lasting effects." He thrust a wooden cup into her hand.

She stared down at the dark liquid, feeling like Juliet. But Andrew was not her Romeo. He had made that perfectly clear.

"Are you sure you're okay with this?" Andrew asked, worry in his voice.

"It's the only way. I was just glad they didn't find anything today." She placed the cup on the ground next to the cot. "Tomorrow they intend to use explosives."

"They won't get the chance even if this doesn't work. I took the explosives."

"Won't that make them suspicious?"

"Probably. I left a jaguar skull as a warning. Remember, they have Indian helpers. I made sure those helpers saw me watching them today."

"Oh, you do have a devilish streak about you."

"I aim to please."

"You do?" She knew the desire and love she felt flowed into him.

He tensed beneath her touch. "Kathleen, I—"

She laid her fingers over his lips. "Shh. I know there can be nothing between us, at least nothing physical. But why can't we come together on a spiritual level? I sense you hold yourself back, that there could be more than there is between us."

He framed her face in his large hands. "Yes, I think there can be, even though I've never done it before."

"What?"

"Meld our minds."

"Like Spock on Star Trek?"

His chuckle rang low and sexy in her ear. "Something like that."

Stunned by the possibility, she couldn't think of anything to say.

"I will know everything there is to know about you. And you will know everything there is to know about me. Do you want to take that kind of chance?"

She had opened herself up to Andrew as she had to no other person, but could she take it all the way and expose herself totally? Everything inside of her cautioned against laying her soul completely bare. How would there be anything left for her to piece back together when she returned to civilization? Years of experience at shielding her feelings demanded she refuse.

"You don't have to answer, Kathleen. I feel your hesitation, and you're right." He pulled away from her caress. "For a moment I wasn't thinking straight. That kind of joining would make it impossible to leave each other. And you must go." He loomed over her in the dark, his features unreadable. "I have to leave."

Tears burned her eyes. She blinked, and several rolled down into her hair. She was glad there was no light in the tent.

"Don't cry," he whispered, brushing away the wet tracks.

"Again I underestimated you. You weren't supposed to see my tears. But then, normal people don't see in the dark like you do."

"I must know that you will be all right."

"Of course. I'm a survivor," she said even though the huge lump in her throat made her question that statement.

"Like me." He backed away. "Good-bye, Kathleen."

She waited until he was gone from the campsite before she let her tears flow freely. A lifetime of tears. A lifetime of pain. She would have to get used to feeling empty in a part of her heart. Some things were never meant to be. She had come to terms with that—at least she thought she had. Until his visit tonight.

She fought the lure of sleep. She didn't want to dream. Sitting up, she bided her time until dawn lightened the sky. Her hands quivering, she brought the wooden cup to her lips.

The potion slid down her throat, soothing some of the tightness. When she had drunk it all, she lifted the canvas at the back of the tent and tossed the cup into the underbrush. She wanted no evidence of what she had done. This had to work.

When she lay down on the cot again, she was already lightheaded. The ceiling spun. She closed her eyes and folded her hands over her chest, waiting for the dark to come.

Chapter Eleven

Andrew perched high up in a tree that overlooked the campsite, waiting for Kathleen's father to find her unconscious. The older man came out of his tent, stretched, and said a few words to his Indian guide. The Indian went off toward the tent that held the box of explosives.

Andrew licked his paw, then rested his head on his extended legs, confident no one from the camp could see him because of the thick foliage.

A few seconds later the guide rushed out of the supply tent, waving the jaguar skull and talking rapidly in Spanish. He hurried over to Dawson, thrusting the skull at him.

"The Jaguar Man is angry with us. We need to leave this place now. People disappear when he's angry."

The older man frowned. "That's a bunch of bull. There is no such thing as a Jaguar Man." His firm, level voice embodied command. "I paid you good money, and you'll do what I want. No questions asked." Dawson took the skull and threw it on the ground.

The guide's eyes widened as he stared at the skull. "No. The men won't take you there."

The Indian's shrill declaration reached Andrew, pleasing him. It had taken years to cultivate this kind of fear, for the myth of the Jaguar Man to spread beyond the rain forest. Just a hint of his anger often sent men scrambling for their canoes. He realized it was easy to frighten the Indians, but Paul Dawson and Dirk Masters were a different matter. It was a challenge he would take if the potion didn't work with Kathleen.

Kathleen's father pushed past the guide and strode to the group of Indians huddled together, talking in low voices and staring wide-eyed at the skull, lying in the dirt. "You tell them that we may not have any explosives, but we will still search today."

"No." The guide shook his head over and over while he backed himself toward his helpers.

"Dammit, you will do what I say."

Andrew smiled inwardly at the sound of Dawson's raised voice. He was losing control. Once that happened it wouldn't be long before everything would fall apart for the expedition.

Dirk Masters appeared from his tent, his face creased with confusion. "What's going on?"

"The explosives are gone. Juan found a jaguar skull in the supply tent. He insists the Jaguar Man is angry, and we can't go any further into the rain forest. He keeps mumbling something about people disappearing."

"I wonder if this is what happened to Kathleen."

"I'll wake her and see. Maybe she has some idea what to do about all this. God knows, I don't." Dawson raked his hand through his hair, showing his frustration in his rigid stance and wrinkled brow.

Andrew moved to a lower branch, still concealed, and watched as Kathleen's father entered her tent.

"Dirk, come here." His shout pierced the quiet of the jungle. "It's Kathleen. She's not moving."

Masters raced to the tent and entered, leaving the flap open so Andrew could see inside. The younger man felt for a pulse.

"She's alive."

"I can't wake her."

Andrew heard the frantic ring in Dawson's voice and decided the man cared for his daughter more than Kathleen realized. Andrew felt a kinship with the older man that he wished he didn't. In the past he had tried hard not to let his emotions get tangled up in what he must do. Kathleen's appearance in the rain forest almost made a mockery of that rule.

"We need to get her to a doctor, Paul."

"That's over a day away. What if she dies before—"

"She won't. She's probably just exhausted."

"To the point of being unconscious? I told her the jungle was full of dangerous things. She wouldn't listen to me."

"We'd better break camp now." Masters came out of the tent and began issuing orders to the Indians to prepare to leave. They jumped to obey.

Dawson picked Kathleen up in his arms and started for the canoes.

"I can help you with her," Masters called out.

"No, she's my responsibility. I'll see to her. You see to everything else. We leave in five minutes."

Satisfied the men were packing up, Andrew descended from the tree and tracked the older man through the jungle to the river. He observed Kathleen's father gently lay her in the first canoe, cushioning her head in his lap. When Andrew looked at the worry on Dawson's face, he knew Kathleen would be in good hands. She would be safe and home soon, living the life she was meant to. And perhaps she would discover her father's love after all.

Within a few minutes the others had loaded the gear into the rest of the canoes, and pushed off into the river. Andrew sat on the shore, the undergrowth protecting him from being seen, and watched Kathleen go out of his life. His heart bled as though someone had stuck a knife into it and twisted the blade.

He was alone again. Yet, jaguars were loners. He was only following nature's course. Then why did he hurt so much?

He roared his protest, realizing the sound carried out over the water. He didn't care. His pain ripped through him and sent him racing along the river's bank, oblivious to the limbs tearing at his fur. He didn't stop until he lost sight of the canoes.

***

The comfortable mattress beneath her was the first thing Kathleen noticed as she surfaced from unconsciousness. The second thing was the cool air caressing her skin, followed quickly by the sounds and smells of a hospital. Their plan had worked!

A sigh trembled from her lips as she eased her eyes open to the bright sunlight streaming through the window. She turned her head toward it and saw her father slumped in a chair next to the bed.

As though he sensed her staring at him, his eyes snapped open, and he straightened. "You're awake."

"Yes, unless this is an elaborate dream. What happened?" She lifted her right hand to touch her head and noticed the IV in her arm.

"The doctors don't know, but then I can guess they don't know a lot about the jungle. They kept muttering about the mysteries of the rain forest." He sat forward in his chair and clasped her left hand. "The important thing is you're awake. How do you feel?"

Surprisingly Andrew had been right. She felt fine, just a little groggy. "Okay. Kinda fuzzy."

"That's to be expected."

What she hadn't expected was her father hovering over her nor the haggard look on his face. "How long have I been here?"

"Only a few hours."

"You look horrible."

He grinned. "Thanks. I didn't get any sleep last night. I was too busy making sure we didn't run into anything on the river. It probably isn't a good idea to navigate a river at night, especially an unfamiliar one."

"Dad, why did you do that?"

"I didn't know what was wrong with you. I had to get you to a doctor."

Her heart expanded at the vehement tone in his voice. He actually sounded like he cared, and the thought that she had been responsible for his pain made her almost regret what she and Andrew had done. But she had had no choice. Dalco couldn't explore for oil in the rain forest, and she had seen this charade as their only way out—at least she hoped so.

"What happened about the oil?" She prayed everyone had come back to the capital.

"Didn't you tell me there wasn't any?"

"Yes."

"Then I see no reason to continue the search. Besides, that area presents a lot of problems."

"What problems?" she asked while relief swept through her.

"For one thing the river floods extensively during the rainy season. And—" He glanced away as though embarrassed.

"What else, Dad?"

"It would be hard to keep workers with that damn myth about the Jaguar Man. Those Indians actually believe there is something like a were-jaguar that kills trespassers in his territory. Of course, there isn't one, but they believe and that's all that matters."

"Yeah, Santo said something about the myth to me. That's the reason he left me there."

"While you were staying with that tribe, did you hear anything else?"

"Yes, many stories. I'm glad to be out of there." Kathleen hunched her shoulders as though chilled.

"You know, sometimes I felt like I was being watched."

"So did I." She shivered again.

"Now, mind you, I don't believe it's the Jaguar Man because there's no such thing as one, but someone definitely didn't want us there and went to a lot of trouble to convince us to leave." He stood, still holding her hand as though he wasn't quite ready to let go of her. "I'm going to get the doctor and tell him you've regained consciousness. As soon as he says you're all right, we're going home."

When her father said the word home, Dallas didn't flash into Kathleen's mind. She thought of Andrew's cavern and the bed of leaves on the platform. She thought of the Indian village and the smiling, trusting faces of the people in it.

"The sooner we leave, the better. I wish I had listened to you and never come here." There was a part of her that believed what she had just said, the empty part that hurt so badly she wasn't sure she would ever be all right again. But then, there was a part of her that would always cherish the time she had spent with Andrew, the love for him she would carry around forever.

"So do I." Her father's grip tightened about her, his gaze fixed on their clasped hands. "I never want to experience that kind of fright again. I thought I had lost you this time. Twice in one week is enough to age me twenty years. The calm safety of Dallas is looking better and better to me."

While her father went to talk with the doctor, Kathleen thought about her life. She had avoided taking risks and had settled for that calm safety her father referred to. And where had it gotten her? She wasn't really happy with what she was doing, and she didn't have many close friends because it was hard for her to trust people. At best, her relationship with her father was strained, and her sister was too busy rebelling to care what happened to the family. When she thought about it, her life was empty, with very few prospects of that changing in the future.

She closed her eyes and tried to imagine her life back in Dallas. She didn't like what she saw. Bleak. Barren.

Then she tried to visualize what it would be like with Andrew by her side. Her heartbeat fluttered at the thought, her pulse quickening. She couldn't shake the feeling that she belonged with him, that without him she would never be whole again.

He didn't want her, had insisted she leave. She understood his reasons. He didn't want to be responsible for her becoming like him. But he hadn't really asked her what she wanted. Now she had to decide what she wanted—needed—to be happy.

The door swished open, and a young man in a white coat came into the room behind her father. The doctor examined her, declared her fit, then left to start the paperwork for her release.

"Good. Now I can make those arrangements for the company plane to pick us up."

"How long do you think it will be?"

"No more than a day."

One day to decide the rest of her life. One day to decide where she truly belonged.

"While you get dressed, I'll make the necessary calls."

When she was alone again, she sat up and swung her legs over the side of the bed. Slowly she rose, grateful when her legs held her up. Before she decided, she needed to talk with her father. She needed answers.

***

"You should be resting, Kathleen," her father said when he entered the hotel suite.

She stood by the picture window, staring at the delta where the river emptied into the sea. That same river led to where Andrew lived. Seeing a boat out in the middle of the water, she wished she were on it, heading into the heart of the jungle.

Her father rested his hand on her shoulder, and she was surprised by the action. He rarely touched her. She liked it, and realized she had missed a lot while growing up. Andrew had awakened in her a desire for the human touch.

"It won't be long before we're back in Dallas and everything will be like before."

His words, meant to reassure, set off an alarm in her mind. She didn't want to live as before. That environment had been cold, sterile, devoid of emotions. She liked how Andrew had made her feel.

She turned toward her father, breaking the connection, but remaining only a foot away. He didn't step back. "Dad, what if I told you I didn't want to go back?"

His brow creased with frown lines. "Why not?"

How could she explain what had happened to her? When she really couldn't explain it to herself? "I've changed, Dad."

"No, you haven't. It's just this place. You've been through a lot these past few weeks."

As usual, he had disregarded what she said and declared what was the truth—at least from his viewpoint. He thought that would be the end of it. Usually it was, but not this time. "I want you to understand before you go home."

His frown deepened. "You make it sound as though you won't be coming."

"I won't be." Upon saying those words out loud, she knew her decision to return to the rain forest and Andrew was the right one. The only one possible for her. She could never be happy in "civilization" if it meant living without him. She would gladly be with him on any terms she could get.

"Nonsense."

"Dad, I need you to listen to *me* for once. I met someone who is living with the Indians. I want to be with him."

"You've gone mad."

"No, quite the opposite. This is the first sane thing I've done for myself. I'll be living the life I want, not one I think you want for me."

"You wanted to be a geologist." His voice rose a level.

"No, you wanted me to be a geologist. I wanted to be a botanist." She decided to take a chance, and reached out to grasp her father's hands. "I spent my whole life trying to be the son you wanted and never quite succeeding because I'm not that son. I want to be your daughter."

"You *are* my daughter."

"Who could never live up to your expectations."

"Is that what you think?"

She waited for him to pull away, but he didn't. The feel of his hands in hers gave her the courage to continue. "Yes. I was never quite good enough. You didn't even come to my high school graduation. I was valedictorian and gave the speech for my class."

"I got delayed with business. I tried to get back to Dallas in time."

"That's just it. I was always second in your life. But it isn't just me. It's the whole family. I don't want work to be my whole life. I want much more than that."

He looked at her as though she had already transformed into a jaguar. "Work is important."

"So is love and family." She squeezed his hands as if that would impart to him how she felt. She thought about the bond she had with Andrew and continued, "I want to experience life to the fullest. I don't expect you to understand my decision, but I felt I needed to try to explain my feelings."

His expression closed, and she hated to see that. She wished just for once he would state how he felt. "Dad, I love you. That won't ever change. But I'm going to live my life the way I want to live it. I'm returning to the rain forest tomorrow morning."

"I can't change your mind?"

"No, but I wish you would give me your support and—" she swallowed the last word, her throat tight with emotions long buried.

"My love?"

She nodded, shocked to hear that word coming from her father's lips.

He stared at her as though memorizing her features. Then he pulled his hands free and wrapped his arms about her, bringing her up against him. "Honey, I've always loved you and your sister."

She laid her head against his chest and listened to his strong heartbeat. She had come home for the first time in her life, and it felt wonderful. "Why didn't you ever tell me?"

"That's not me. I thought you understood that."

She thought of all those years wasted, wondering what her father really felt. That realization made her regret what could have been. He couldn't express his emotions; she had been the same way. Andrew had taught her to feel. Until him, Kathleen hadn't realized how much she had missed.

Her father pulled back. "Who is this man who is stealing my daughter?"

"His name is Guerriro." It wasn't her place to let the world know that Andrew Stone was alive. If her father knew, he would tell others.

"What kind of name is that? His first name? Last?"

"First and last. He goes by Guerriro. He is studying the Indian tribe who lives in the area."

"Is he an anthropologist?"

"No."

"Then I don't understand."

"There's nothing to understand. He works with the Indians to help them preserve their way of life."

"A missionary?"

"Yes." *Of sorts*, she added silently.

He shook his head. "I can't picture you living the life of a missionary. You realize you'll be living in primitive conditions. Kathleen, have you really thought this through?"

"Yes, I know how I'll be living." When she pictured herself standing next to Andrew on top of the cliff overlooking the rain forest, she felt peace settling over her.

"Then there's nothing I can say to change your mind?"

"No."

He leaned over and kissed her forehead. "Just remember I—" He swallowed hard. "I love you, Kathleen."

Tears stung her eyes. "I love you, too."

***

Kathleen sat on a fallen tree trunk next to the tent she had erected. She smiled when she remembered her guide letting her off at the riverbank and being told to leave. He had hesitated until she assured him she was expected by the Indian tribe in the area and would be perfectly fine.

Now she would wait for Andrew to come. She knew he would. Perhaps not right away, but he wouldn't leave her there alone for long.

She drew in a deep breath of the moisture-laden air and felt at home. All around her were various shades of green with sprinkles of color from different flowers that grew on the trees. She heard the distance cry of a howler monkey and recalled her first night in Andrew's cavern when Zenna's pet monkey had been there.

Darkness descended quickly. She lit the lantern and continued to wait, no longer afraid of the night, of the black shadows. One of them was Andrew. She could sense his presence nearby.

He had come.

All she had to do was convince him she wanted to stay and be his mate more than anything in this world, even if it meant becoming a Jaguar Woman. The next hour would be the most important hour of her life.

Minutes crawled by, and still he kept himself hidden in the dark.

"I won't go away," she called out in the direction she knew he was.

He emerged from the shadows, striding toward her with long, angry steps. His hands were fisted at his sides, and even from across the camp, she felt his vehement emotions. He came to a halt several feet from her, his face illuminated by the lantern light, his gaze unyielding.

"Why did you come back, Kathleen? No good will come of this. I only have so much willpower."

Even though his voice was calm, she sensed the immovable power behind his words. "I belong here with you."

"No." He practically roared the declaration.

"Don't I have a say in my life?"

"No."

"I love you, Andrew. Leaving will not change that. *Ever*."

He flinched as though she had hit him. "Kathleen, this isn't for you." He waved his hand in the air, gesturing to the jungle.

Her own anger grew, and she allowed it to, reveling in the freedom she felt in expressing it. "What gives you the right to decide what is best for me? I just walked away from a life where I lived someone else's expectations of me. Never again. Now it is *my* turn to do what *I* want."

"Disregarding my wants?"

"I'm not disregarding your wants." She reached out and grasped his hand, feeling the immediate bond. A jolt of desire streaked through her, their emotions entwining, fusing. It was the most wonderful feeling in the world. "I want to stay. And if you are true to what you feel, you want that, too."

His eyes darkened, a nerve twitching in his clenched jaw. "No, that's not possible. You know what will happen to you. I can't put you through that. Don't put any more guilt on me."

"I want to be put through that. We can race through the jungle together. We can protect the Indians together. We can make love throughout the night." She saw the softening in the harsh lines of his face. "Do you love me?"

He blinked, surprise evident in his expression.

"Do you?" Her grip on his arm tightened, their flow of emotions continuing to link them.

He looked away, over her shoulder, a war battling within him. She felt his tension, his confusion, his desire. Her grip loosened, and she stroked him as though that would ease his struggle.

"You know I can't deny it. You feel what I feel, so you know I love you," he finally answered, his gaze returning to her face. "But that doesn't change the situation."

"That changes everything, Andrew." Her arms encircled him and drew him flush against her. His reply was silenced by the pressure of her mouth against his, her tongue slipping inside to savor his sweet flavor.

Molding herself even more into his hard planes, she increased the force of her kiss, wanting to make him see he couldn't live without her. She was a part of him—as much as his heart, his very soul—and she flowed through his veins, as essential to his survival as his blood.

She ran her hands up his back and buried her fingers in the long strands of his hair, enjoying the silky feel that slipped through her grasp. She plundered his mouth, seeking to brand him as hers. Just as she was beginning to feel she had succeeded, he wrenched himself from her embrace and distanced himself.

"This doesn't change a thing, Kathleen." His chest rose and fell rapidly. "This isn't you." Again his gesture encompassed the rain forest. "How long do you think you would last before you became bored by all this? You would start to hate me, and if we mated, the promise I am forced to keep, you would be forced to keep. You're meant for civilization. Your home is in Dallas."

She took one step toward him, then another. "Yes, I have an apartment in Dallas, but it isn't a home. It's four walls and a roof over my head. My so-called life is getting up six days a week, eating breakfast, driving to work, staying at my desk for twelve, sometimes thirteen, hours a day then driving home, fixing a dinner and falling into bed. Yeah, I'd say that was an exciting, adventurous life. One I should fight for." She reached to grasp his arms, needing to feel his connection.

He backed away, putting up his hands as if to stop her from advancing. "I'm having Bonito take you to the capital."

Tilting her chin at a defiant angle, she crossed her arms and braced herself. "No."

His eyes narrowed. "I have my ways. I can make you go."

"I'll just come back until you accept that I'm here to stay."

He combed his fingers through his hair, frustration apparent in his jerky movements.

She covered the few remaining feet between them and gripped his arms, compelling him to look at her. "Do you feel it? I love you more than life itself. I want to spend my days and nights with you. If your promise to these people keeps you here, then it keeps me here, too. Your promise is my promise because we are two halves of a whole."

"No, my pledge isn't yours."

She cradled his face in her hands. "Yes, it is. We are one. I've never in my life felt this way about another. From the first, the connection between us was undeniable. I fought it. You fought it. But it survived because it is stronger than both of us. Together we can do anything, overcome any obstacle. Apart we'll shrivel up and die a little bit each day we're separated. I know this here." She placed his hand over her heart. "You're my soul mate."

The harsh lines on his face vanished as she held his hand against her breast, letting her love shower him with its intensity, its passion.

"I never thought another would desire this life, and I can't walk away from it." He shook his head as though not quite believing she wanted to stay with him, wanted to become like him. "Are you sure? Once we make love—"

She placed her fingers against his mouth to quiet his words. "Since I came to the rain forest, I have experienced life to the fullest. You're the reason for that. I wasn't living in

Dallas. I was merely existing." She wrapped her arms around him and fused herself against his length. "Anyone can exist. Not everyone can really feel, taste, see, hear her surroundings like I have since I arrived here."

His tension melted completely away, and he captured her mouth in a driving kiss while he held her in his arms. When they came up for air, he said, "There's so much I want to show you. There are ancient Indian ruins yet undiscovered...a waterfall and pool that I swear are what the Garden of Eden looked like. And the animals and plants. Whole species yet unknown to all except the natives."

"And we'll start tomorrow. Tonight I want you to make love to me until dawn breaks. This is the first night of the rest of our lives—together. I want to hold on to this night. I want to meld minds with you. I'm not afraid anymore. I want you to know everything there is to know about me, to the darkest recesses of my mind."

He held his hand out to her. "Then come. Let's go home."

***

When she entered the large cavern, she felt complete, as though she was finally being true to herself—had finally truly come home. She closed her eyes and savored the moment of contentment.

Andrew came up behind her and drew her back against him. "I love you, Kathleen."

If she had any fear of the future, those simple words wiped all doubts from her mind. "I love you, Andrew." She turned in his arms and placed her palms against his. "Can you feel it?"

He laced their fingers together and yanked her up against him. "Yes."

Slanting his mouth across hers, he took hers in a deep kiss that made her clutch him for support as her world spun. He backed her across the cavern, all the while his tongue parried with hers. When her legs hit the platform and she stopped, he scooped her up in his arms and laid her on the bed of leaves with such tenderness that her heart swelled. He quickly followed her down, stretching his long length beside hers.

"I want you inside of me, Andrew. *Now.* We've waited long enough."

"That's the only place I want to be."

He covered her body with his, moving like a jaguar, sure and swift. He stripped away her clothes and, with one lunge entered her, filling her completely. Pausing deep inside, he cupped her face in his large hands and crushed his lips down upon hers, his tongue sweeping into her mouth. Then he began his thrusts, hard and fast, expanding her beyond what she thought possible, making her totally and forever his.

As they climaxed, his male essence suffused her, his emotions uniting with hers and becoming one. The overwhelming intensity of the moment seized her breath. Never before had she joined another so completely, physically and emotionally. She knew him as no one else, and he knew her. She had come home.

When she regained some semblance of composure, she shifted in his embrace, laying her head on his chest to listen to this heartbeat. The slowing rhythm matched hers, as did their meshing emotions. When they had come together, it had truly been as one in mind, body and soul. That realization stunned her. She had been lost in him and he in her.

"I've never felt this way," she whispered, awed that she could know another person so well.

"Neither have I." He stroked her arm, which lay on his chest. "The shaman doesn't even know how to explain this connection we have. I don't know if he will be happy that you returned."

She reached up and touched his face. "I don't want to talk about him. I want you again."

"This time it's for you." He came up to kneel beside her on the large bed.

His hand skimmed the length of her in a feather light touch that primed her for him, making her quiver in anticipation. She wasn't sure what he intended, but she knew he would never hurt her. He stopped his exploration and caressed her womanhood, one finger then two slipping inside. She nearly came up off the bed as his hand continued to plunge into her. Then suddenly he stopped and began to kiss her breast, taking a nipple into his mouth and sucking. When he trailed tiny nips over her stomach and kissed her where his hand had been, Kathleen gripped his hair. His tongue lathed her and sent her arching up into his kisses as her world, a myriad of sensations, all centered on Andrew.

He had only one desire, to please her. Her satisfaction would become his. He reined in his passion, even though he was hard with need for her, and relished her taste on his lips, his tongue. She writhed beneath him, her moans prodding him toward his own release. He restrained himself with an ironclad effort he hadn't thought possible, which hadn't been possible before her.

Kathleen soared through the heavens, flying high above the rain forest, her body awash in unbelievable sensations. She dug her fingernails into his shoulders and brought him up to kiss her. Sampling herself on his lips, she marveled at the total surrender she experienced in his arms.

She pushed him onto his back and began nibbling on his flesh. She traveled lower, then took him into her mouth, bathing him with kisses meant to drive him crazy with desire for her. She loved the feel of him in her hands as she straddled him and guided him inside. Slowly she began to slide up and down him, not wanting to rush, wanting to prolong every delicious second of their mating. Suddenly, he grasped her hips and compelled her to move faster.

He cried out her name while they climaxed again. Shudder after shudder shook her body. She collapsed on top of him, breathing in shallow gasps. Her pulse sped, sweeping reality away and leaving in its place a dream-like rapture.

Exhausted, she nestled in his embrace, letting the darkness of the cavern soothe her. She felt sleep inch closer and finally surrendered to it as she had to Andrew—totally, with no reservations.

***

Andrew cradled Kathleen to him, still stunned that she would want to share his life. But he had no doubts—not after the past few hours uniting with her on several levels. There were no secrets between them now. He knew her as well as he knew himself. He loved her even more.

His tongue flicked the corners of her mouth. "Wake up, sleepyhead. Dawn's approaching."

She stretched, her eyes slowly opening. "Let's greet the dawn out on the cliff."

Her eagerness touched him. His mouth covered hers again, tasting her sweetness. "Then we'd better hurry."

He took her hand and led her through the maze to the ledge from which she had fallen days before. With her hand still within his, he faced the east and saw the beginnings of the dawn tinge the sky pearl gray.

They waited side by side, the silence of the new day comforting. Pink fingered outward, pushing its way through the gray.

"I don't feel any different, Andrew."

"Neither do I," he said, puzzled that he didn't.

Dawn brightened the sky.

Andrew lifted his arm and looked down at it. "I don't understand. We should have transformed by now."

Kathleen turned toward him, taking his face in her hands. "Is the spell broken somehow?"

He shook his head. "The only thing different is that we made love last night."

She smiled. "Just as I was looking forward to racing through the jungle with you."

A movement out of the corner of his eye caught his attention. The shaman emerged from the cave. Kathleen stepped behind Andrew, conscious of the fact she was naked.

"What's happened?" Andrew asked him in his language.

"Love has freed you. Your debt has been paid." The small man disappeared into the shadows.

"What is it?" Kathleen asked, concern in her expression.

"I'm free," Andrew murmured, still amazed by the news, remembering the shaman's warning about Kathleen. The old Indian had been afraid of her power over him. He had known what would happen. "We're free."

"To leave?"

"If we want."

"What if we want to stay a while?"

"We can." Andrew clasped Kathleen's shoulders and stared down at her beautiful face. "Do you want to?"

"Yes. Your job isn't done."

He buried his fingers in her hair and kissed her, long, hard. "Thank you for understanding I can't leave just yet. These people are important to me."

"They're important to me, too."

Turning, they both looked eastward, Andrew slipping his arm about Kathleen's shoulders and bringing her up against him. As a man, it had been five years since he had felt sunlight on his face. He lifted it up and basked in the warmth, glorying in his future with Kathleen by his side as his mate.

ABOUT THE AUTHOR

Shauna Michaels, aka Margaret Ripy and Kit Daley, is a multi-published author with thirty books in the romance genre. She has been writing romances for the past twenty years. She has written for Dell, Silhouette, Kensington, Starlight Writer Publications, and ImaJinn Books. She has mostly written contemporary romances but has done two historicals and one paranormal, *Hold onto the Night*.

Shauna is fortunate enough to be married to the same man for the last twenty-nine years and has one son who is in college right now. She has always felt her husband is her inspiration in life and love and draws on her marriage to write her love stories.

When Shauna isn't working on a book or teaching students with disabilities, she loves to read romances, go to the movies with friends, and travel. She has traveled to many places in the world from South America to Europe. She likes to use these locations in her books. *Hold onto The Night* is placed in a jungle. She had the pleasure of visiting a rain forest in Belize a few years back.

Shauna loves to hear from her readers. You can contact her at P. O. Box 2074, Tulsa, OK, 74101 or you can visit her web site at:

http://members.aol.com/APR427/.

Current and
Upcoming Releases
From
Imajinn Books

February 2000

Mad About Max by Holly Fuhrmann. Retail Price: $8.50. Description: Fantasy Romance; an author's fictional three fairy godmother characters come to life and proceed to find her a Prince Charming. This is the first book in the fairy godmother trilogy.

March 2000

Cupid: The Bewildering Bequest by J. M. Jeffries. Retail Price: $8.50. Description: Fantasy Romance. Jason Stavros and Merrill Prescott have become co-guardians of a dog who just inherited $75 million. But Cupid and Venus are determined to match-make Jason and Merrill, despite the fact that Jupiter has decided to make Merrill his latest conquest. This is the second book in what will be a continuing "Cupid" series from J. M. Jeffries.

April 2000

Timeless Shadows by J. A. Ferguson. Retail Price: $9.95. Description: Time travel romance with a touch of magic and witchcraft; the heroine goes back in time and discovers that she'd been sent forward in time when she was a baby. Now she's swept back in time to (English) Civil War Scotland where she may be the way to save what was her family's castle or the cause of its destruction.

May 2000

Midnight Gamble by Nancy Gideon. Retail Price: $9.95. Description: Fantasy romance; this is the second book in the

"Midnight" vampire romance trilogy to be released by ImaJinn Books. The first book was released in December, 1999

June 2000

Etched in Stone by Dimitri Eann. Retail Price: $9.95. Description: Time travel romance; the heroine goes back to ancient Egypt, only to learn that she's come back to a previous life where she murdered the man whom she'll love forever. Can she save his life and change history that has been etched in stone for 4000 years?

July 2000

Hold Onto the Night by Shauna Michaels. Retail Price: $9.95. Description: Fantasy romance; the hero is a shapeshifter who, as a black jaguar by day and a man by night, guards the rain forest from men who seek to destroy it.

August 2000

Dreamshaper by J. A. Ferguson. Retail Price: $9.95. Description: Fantasy romance; this is the second book in the "Dream" trilogy. The first book, ***Dreamsinger*** was released in October, 1999.

September 2000

Last Hope by Chloe Hall. Retail Price: $9.95. Description: Science Fiction romance. Arkana Swallowsong has just married Connall Storm because he's agreed to help find out what happened to her parents when they ventured into the wilderness more than 20 years ago. Connall is certain that by finding Arkana's parents he'll be able to increase his wealth. But as they follow the path Arkana's parents took into the wilderness, they unexpectedly discover love and a dark secret about their adopted planet that will destroy the entire human population.

October 2000
(1st Anniversary Month)

Arabian Nights by Tracy Cozzens. Retail Price: $9.95. Description: Fantasy time travel romance; a wheelchair bound heroine releases a genie from a bottle. As one of her three wishes, she wishes the genie to be free. Her wish sweeps them back in time to when the hero was first turned into a genie, and they must battle the evil Ifrit to free the hero from his genie curse.

Midnight Redeemer by Nancy Gideon. Retail Price: $9.95. Description: Fantasy romance; this is the third in the "Midnight" vampire romance trilogy to be released by ImaJinn Books. The first book was released in December, 1999, and the second book was released in May, 2000.

November 2000

Magic for Joy by Holly Fuhrmann. Retail Price: $8.50. Description: Fantasy romance. Joy Aaronson and Gabriel St. John seem to have only one thing in common–they both love Gabriel's six-year-old daughter Sophie. But the three fairy godmother's are convinced that Gabriel is Joy's Prince Charming. They just have to convince Joy of that! This is the second book in the "Fairy Godmother" trilogy. The first book, ***Mad About Max*** was released in February 2000.

December

Glass Slipper.com by Rebecca Anderson. Retail Price: $8.50. Description: Fantasy romance; the witches of Wishmakers, Inc., must find the perfect husband for a clutzy, computer-nerd heroine before the beginning of the real new millennium (January 1st, 2001), or Wishmakers will be disbanded.

NOTE: The above publishing schedule is subject to change.

ORDER FORM

Name:_____

Address:_____

City:_____

State___Zip_____ Phone*_____

Qty	Book	Cost	Amount

Total Paid by:	SUBTOTAL	
☐ Check or money order	SHIPPING	
☐ Credit Card (Circle one) Visa Mastercard Discover American Express	MI Residents add 6% sales tax	
_____ _Card Number	TOTAL	

_____
Expiration Date

_____
Name on Card

Would you like your book(s) autographed? If so, please provide the name the author should use_____

*Phone number is required if you pay by Credit Card

Shipping costs:
1 book $2.00
Each additonal book $.50
(Shipping prices for U.S. residents only. Foreign customers will be notified if we can ship to your country, and we'll get your approval of shipping charges prior to filling your order)

MAIL TO: ImaJinn Books, PO Box 162, Hickory Corners, MI 49060-0162

Visit our web site at: http://www.imajinnbooks.com

Questions? Call us toll free: 1-877-625-3592